URGENT MATTERS

paula rodríguez

TRANSLATED FROM THE SPANISH BY SARAH MOSES

PUSHKIN
VERTIGO

Pushkin Vertigo
An imprint of Pushkin Press
Somerset House, Strand
London WC2R 1LA

Urgent Matters was first published as *Causas urgentes* by Alfaguara in 2020

First published by Pushkin Press in 2022

Work published within the framework of "Sur" Translation Support Program
of the Ministry of Foreign Affairs and Worship of the Argentine Republic

Obra editada en el marco del Programa "Sur" de Apoyo a las Traducciones
del Ministerio de Relaciones Exteriores y Culto de la República Argentina

1 3 5 7 9 8 6 4 2

ISBN 13: 978-1-78227-815-3

Designed and typeset by Tetragon, London
Printed and bound by Clays Ltd, Elcograf S.p.A.

www.pushkinpress.com

PUSHKIN
VERTIGO

URGENT MATTERS

'[A] breathless procedural… a notable addition to South American noir'

Times and *Sunday Times* Crime Club Pick of the Week

'A vivid and unforgiving depiction of a world in which everyone… is guilty of something'

Guardian

'Written in the taut, clean style of the classic pulp noir… the story barrels along at a ferocious rate'

Irish Times

'Part thriller, part telenovela… all Argentine in its awareness of how society makes accommodation with corruption'

Times (Best Thrillers of November 2022)

'Fast-paced and funny, breathing life into a disparate and intriguing cast of characters'

Alison Flood, *Guardian*

'This fast-moving novel evokes the teeming metropolis of Buenos Aires in a vibrant fashion… affording alluring insights into a country still divided by class and race'

Crime Time

'Frenetic pace and a hypnotic, disturbing plot… in the post-truth era, it is an essential read'

Agustina Bazterrica, author of *Tender is the Flesh*

'As capable of irony as tenderness, of social and cultural critique as moments of intimacy, and loaded with the frenetic pace of noir'

Gabriela Cabezón Cámara, author of the International Booker-shortlisted *The Adventures of China Iron*

'It has all the ingredients of the police procedurals that totally grip you. It's fast-paced, has action, suspense and great characters'

Claudia Piñeiro, International Booker-shortlisted author of *Elena Knows*

PAULA RODRÍGUEZ is a journalist, editor, writer, comedian, ghostwriter and feminist activist. She has worked for twenty-five years in magazine print journalism. *Urgent Matters* is her first novel. Paula lives in Buenos Aires.

SARAH MOSES is a writer and translator of French and Spanish. She co-translated *Die, My Love* by Ariana Harwicz, which was longlisted for the International Booker Prize, among other awards. Her translation of Agustina Bazterrica's *Tender is the Flesh* was published by Pushkin Press in 2020.

To the journalist I dreamt of becoming.

...you and me, we got the obligation
to stand up for hundreds, thousands, tens of thousands
of people who can't follow the fine points.

TOM WOLFE, *Back to Blood*

The dead don't take the bus.

– *A journalism school saying*

PART ONE

D UST RAISED by the impact falls slowly onto the bodies. The thickest particles are struck by a shaft of light, and amid the sparkling dust, a St Expeditus holy card hangs suspended in the air and in a silence that could mean life or death. Expeditus flutters over the heads, doesn't decide on any of them. Because who isn't a shit in the end? He seems to be enjoying the suspense. Then, suddenly, he floats upwards, collides with the roof, flips face down and takes a nosedive towards Hugo, the highest point on a mountain of bodies. Hugo's hand reaches for the holy card, his neck twisted in the direction of Buenos Aires, facing the barrio of Liniers like the other bodies, which are piled up, jumbled together, crushed against the walls of the carriage, spilling out the window, dislocated, broken, busted.

Hugo grabs hold of the patron saint of urgent matters. His arms are outstretched, the holy card in one hand, his mobile in the other. The soft bodies are clambering onto him, and he digs his elbows into one of them, pushing it down to free himself, so he can breathe. "Sorry," he says, but no one answers. He can't feel his legs and he's afraid. It's no longer silent. People are coughing, moaning, creaking, crying. A draft of air and some sounds make their way in from outside. Hugo hopes the firefighters have arrived. He pleads with Expeditus, asking to be taken out first. The people praying make him even more anxious. He wishes they would shut up and die already.

Hugo also deals with urgent situations. As a locksmith. He'd been on his way to the barrio of Once to help some bloke locked in an office. The man had stayed late to finish his work. Now Hugo won't be able to get him out. This is what he gets for not taking the 163 bus like Marta told him. Just as things were going better between them, this had to happen. If he dies, Marta will be saying "I told you so" for the rest of her life. But she's wrong. It's just chance. Same goes with salvation—it's random. No one's saved because they pray to God or cry to a saint. Someone needs to call the firefighters.

There's a message on Hugo's phone and the screen lights up a shattered face. It's the old lady who got on with him in the suburbs at Ituzaingó. Her eyes were already bulging a bit then. She was pushing a girl out of the way to get a seat. That girl must now be under her. Hugo feels about with his feet. The carriage is still dark but he's beginning to make out the shapes of the shadows. He tries to read the WhatsApp message without looking around him. There are several dead, he knows this without seeing the bodies. He knows it because of the smell, which has been following him. It's a smell he now recognizes easily based on what it's not: it's not like flesh or fear or rot. Instead, it's like the smell of recently cut grass, a euphoric smell.

The message is from Marta:

Come home it's urgent

Marta never says why. That's what she's like, alarmist. Everything is urgent. She's probably watching the Turkish soap. And wanting to irritate him. Why won't she put the news on to see what happened with the train? Hugo types out: "you come here, Marta." It's not that seeing her or saying goodbye feels urgent; it's his anger at getting messages like this. She wants to have him by the balls, to make him feel he owes her something, while he's the one suffocating. How long will he have to wait? How long can a person bear this? Before Hugo is able to send the message, he gets another one from Marta. The startled face of the dead old lady lights up again.

The police are looking for you

As though they were in cahoots with Marta, a couple of blokes with flashlights turn up. They direct the beams inside the carriage. Hugo is blinded and closes his eyes. There are sirens, voices, the sounds of people running. So much for St Expeditus. It's all a bunch of lies.

"I'm no saint, but neither are you."

Hugo is talking to the holy card. Though he's not sure whether he thinks these words or says them out loud. There's a lot of noise now. And people screaming. No one is listening from the beyond. And if someone is, who are they going to listen to first? A billion people are praying louder than Hugo, people more likely to make it into heaven than him and everyone else in the carriage. You go when your time's up and not because there's some capo pointing at you from above. There's no need for a God who punishes or a figure on a flimsy card who demands you repent in order to be saved. Hugo has already repented. He's not innocent but he's "not guilty". He thinks this in English, just like in the movies, which is what Beto says with an odd look and a smirk when the two of them go over what happened. Hugo says "what we did", but Beto corrects him and says "what happened". Beto's no saint either. The Yankees are more astute when it comes to matters like these. They say "not guilty". They don't say "innocent". Because as far as innocence goes, no one can make that claim.

Where are you

Marta doesn't use question marks. Or full stops, or commas, or any other punctuation. She's a highly anxious person. So Hugo erases what he wrote and quickly, he replies:

Sorry, I fucked up.
√/

E VELYN NEARLY DIES of fright when the police enter her home. She jumps off the couch and freezes. It's a good thing a shot has just been fired—the police think that's the reason. There are two of them, her mum let them in. The sound of the second bullet has all three of them looking at the television. Kerem is lying in the street, his white shirt stained with blood. Bennu is talking to him on his mobile, saying she loves him. He hears her but can't respond and stretches out an arm, tries to reach the phone that has fallen onto the pavement. It's night, there's no one around to help Kerem, and Bennu keeps talking, unaware that her husband is dying. Evelyn watches the soap without moving, without breathing. She feigns not having heard the doorbell, not having seen them come in. If you don't look at them, they won't look at you, she thinks; if you keep still, they won't see you. Her heart about to explode, Evelyn stands there repeating, ohmygod, ohmygod, ohmygod. She thinks quickly about what she'll do if they take her to the station, if she's arrested, if she misses her graduation trip, if it would be best to confess and apologize. Like the principal said, ohmygod, she was yelling so much. It's better to confess and apologize because either way the police will find the fingerprints and in less than a day they'll know who stole Miss Laura's mobile.

Evelyn is guilty. Even if her mum were to tell the police that wasn't possible, that there must be a mistake. She already has a tablet, but she wanted a mobile so she could join the WhatsApp group Martín's in and chat with him. And then everything went wrong because Miss Laura found out right away and she had them queue up in the courtyard and she threatened to go through their backpacks. Evelyn almost confessed. She didn't because the principal was screaming loads and it would have been so embarrassing, way more embarrassing than if the police handcuffed her now and took her to the station in front of the whole neighbourhood, way more than if her mum yanked her by the hair and forced her to turn around and asked, whatdidyoudonow?

But none of this happens because the police leave without a search. Evelyn and her mum hear the sound of their pickup. Now is the time to save themselves. Before the police come back with reinforcements. Her mum is calm in the kitchen. They could flee, go to Brazil, change their names. Evelyn could call herself Carmina.

DETECTIVE DOMÍNGUEZ reads on his phone what he already suspects: the bloke they're looking for isn't at the 163 bus stop. Of course he's not. Domínguez gets up without saying anything, and prepares to leave without giving an explanation. He hasn't been seated in the dining room for more than ten minutes. Marta hasn't even offered him a glass of water.

"Have a good evening, ma'am," he says on his way out and hands her a card. "This is my mobile number. Anything comes up, you let me know."

Not that she will. That much is clear to Domínguez as he heads for the pickup, the neighbours' eyes on the back of his neck. "We'll decide how to proceed tomorrow," he says to no one, looking at the empty street in the rearview mirror before he starts the engine. The Toyota is the latest model and he has ten blocks to enjoy it alone before picking up Ramírez and stopping by Haedo Station. His body is taking him there, though there's no need for a homicide detective at the scene of an accident. He turns on the air conditioning and drives at twenty to draw out the moment and allow his intuitions to form an intelligible shape.

In the kitchen, Marta hears the engine start and calculates how long it will take Domínguez to reach the corner. It's only then that she gets moving. She places the police officer's card in the pocket of her jeans and turns off the television. Evelyn gets scared more easily than she used to, but she holds her mother's gaze.

"Empty your backpack, bring me your folders. Hurry up."

On her bed, Marta places two large towels, two sets of single sheets, one pair of jean shorts, one sweater, one fleece jacket, three long-sleeve shirts, three with short sleeves, a couple of leggings, one pair of sneakers. She puts fifteen grand inside the backpack. Ten in her bra. Five on top of the clothes. She empties the nightstand and separates out her eyeglasses, their ID cards, Evelyn's birth certificate. Marta thinks quickly. Two minutes and you've got someone who's not right in the head figured out, Hugo told her when they were students. He thinks more slowly than she does but he acts faster. That's why they're always going nowhere. Hugo because he's impulsive and Marta out of habit.

She's not hesitating now, she's carrying out the evacuation plan as though she'd rehearsed it. Tonight, the clarity with which she sees things has moved down into her body. She loses control just once, when she can't find their travel bag. She even roots around in the back of the closet. But the huge bag isn't there, the one Hugo always makes an idiotic joke about, saying he'll force Evelyn into it so they won't have to pay her fare. Eventually Evelyn starts crying and everything ends badly. It's a Nike bag with the Barça crest printed on it, not like the embroidered original. That's how the first police officer to leave described it, to see if it rang a bell for Marta. That bag. It's not there. They'll have to make do with a small suitcase.

Evelyn comes over with her school folders. Marta opens them on the bed, takes out the sheets Evelyn has written on, and puts them in a pile. Maths on the bottom, on top of that Spanish, then social sciences and natural sciences.

"Go get your books and pencil case. Pick out your favourite clothes. I'll explain later. Hurry up now and don't worry."

The double bed is a jumble of clothes, money and empty folders. Romeo Santos, the King of Bachata, is smiling sideways on the Spanish and social sciences folders.

"Can I take this with me?" Evelyn asks, and it's clear she's understood her mother's instructions. She promises herself it's the last time she'll open her mouth that night.

"No, please hurry. Give me the tablet."

Evelyn's eyes fill with tears.

"I'll give it to you tomorrow," Marta promises.

They leave without making any noise, the lights left on, the door unlocked. They practically break into a run on their way to Ituzaingó Station. Marta is silent and looks at WhatsApp from time to time. Evelyn is panting behind her mother, her hands in the pockets of her new jacket, the bachata star's photo rescued sneakily during the exodus and Miss Laura's mobile at the very bottom of her backpack.

Evelyn tries to breathe deeply so she can get enough air. That's what she does in gym class when she's forced to run.

Inhale exhale, ohmygod ohmygod, inhale exhale, ohmygod ohmygod, inhale exhale. There was this girl who'd been forced to run so much she died. Evelyn can't stop thinking about her: she saw the video on YouTube. The girl had been punished by her grandma for eating some pastries. She kept saying she didn't feel well, but her grandma was so angry she didn't listen. Evelyn's mum doesn't look angry, all she said was to be quiet. "Be quiet, Evelyn, and please hurry up. Run, Evelyn. Don't worry." But Evelyn is worried.

She wants to die, to cry, but crying makes things worse. With her mum it's better not to. She feels the sausages they had for dinner in her throat. Her mum is holding her hand tightly and not looking at her. They walk very quickly and when they reach the station, they're out of breath. It's that her mum wants to save her and has forgotten about her dad. What will he do if he's left by himself? Evelyn really wants to ask, but it's better not to bring up the subject. Come on, you can do it, she says to herself, tell Mum you don't want to leave and then deal with the punishment. Start secondary school at a juvenile detention centre, get a tattoo. That's better than running to death and leaving without Dad. It's better than waiting with a suitcase and money at a dark station where you might get robbed and anything could happen, where you could get killed for a mobile.

In her head, Evelyn recites the list of students in 7B at her school, Los Santos Ángeles Custodios. Marta looks through her WhatsApp contacts. Hugo hasn't sent her any more messages. The train isn't coming. Marta writes to Mónica:

I'm on my way to yours

✓✓

With evelyn

✓✓

Should be there at five

✓✓

I'll explain later

✓✓

She takes 500 out of her bra and crosses over to the Belgrano taxi stand. They don't know her and Evelyn there.

Evelyn follows behind, relieved. There are a lot of people in the street. The air is cooler after the hot day. Cars drive by with the windows down and the music turned up. They're playing the songs people will be dancing to in the summer. Some of the shops are still open. Marta speaks to her daughter for the first time since they left their house.

"Don't ask me for anything, we've already started spending our cash."

Evelyn buries her chin in the neck of her jacket. She doesn't plan on asking for anything. Ever again.

MYJESUS, pardon and mercy, through the merits of your holy wounds. Mónica repeats this ten times, and with two fingers in her waistcoat pocket, she touches her rosary beads, her steps following the prayer's rhythm as she walks along a red carpet with a design that's yellow but looks like gold. Mónica is very religious. When it comes to God, Christ and the Virgin—the important figures. Marta's the one who's into the saints. Mónica is the believer and worshipper. She walks along the border on the floor, with its Egyptian designs, and when she reaches the corner, she recites in her head, I offer you the wounds ofourlordjesuschrist to heal the wounds of our souls. She turns left and begins again with myjesus, pardon and mercy, then walks along the corridor between the hypnotic sounds and the fantastical creatures, unicorns, exotic dancers, Ramses's treasures, muscular gladiators. They're all in attendance tonight. Mónica can't see their faces but by now she recognizes them from behind. Each at their favourite slot machine. Some of them cross themselves, kiss little medallions, crucifixes. This isn't faith. It's the desire to save yourself.

Why would anyone have a mega jackpot on a Monday night? It's as busy as a Friday. The only calm day of the week and they have to make it a mega jackpot. And Marta has to show up out of nowhere with Evelyn. The rosary helps time go by faster. Every so often someone interrupts to ask her about the progressive jackpot. Why do they play if they don't understand? The man at the Double Dragon machine has already come over three times to tell her it didn't pay him enough. The machine doesn't make mistakes. Mónica can tell it's going to end badly. As for the situation between Marta and Hugo—she saw that coming. She wanders among the wounds of incurable souls and sends WhatsApp messages:

Does Mum know?

√√

Marta's not going to like the question but Mónica wants to be prepared. When it comes to their mother, she's not afraid of Hugo. He's just a poor wretch. She does another lap around the main hall, repeating the rosary in her head again. Though she could shout it out—it's so noisy no one would hear her. When she reaches the mysteries, she looks at her phone. I offer you the wounds ofourlordjesuschrist to heal the wounds of our souls. Marta has seen the message but she's not answering. She must be angry.

"Throughtheholywounds!" Mónica says, this time out loud because the man is now kicking the Double Dragon machine and she has to call security before he breaks it.

The incident dispels the bad thoughts.

"Have you heard about the train?" asks the taxi driver. Marta answers drily that she has not and stares at her phone. There's a message from Mónica. And not one from Hugo. Typical of him. He's waiting for Marta to say something but she doesn't know what. She's not in the mood to order her thoughts, to look for words. Real endings aren't conversations, they're facts. Things you can't say clearly but that you carry out with certainty. Words slip away over the years. At first, you say them all. But over time, they get stuck in your throat, in your stomach, in some part of your body. Then they fade and they're no longer a burden.

"What I think is that if Kerem dies it's better."

Evelyn's voice shakes Marta from her thoughts. She'd forgotten they were fleeing together.

"What?"

"That it's better for Bennu, for Scheherazade, for Onur…"

"But you want him to die? He's not that bad."

"It's good for everyone, Mum." Now that she has her mother's attention, Evelyn asks, "What about Dad?"

"We'll talk later."

Evelyn opens the window, rests her head against the seat. Travelling at night puts her in a state of expectation. It's like being grown-up and free, floating along at high speeds with the wind blowing in your hair in the back seat of a car after a party or driving to the airport on the way to Disneyland. Trips home, on the other hand, always seem to take place during the day. Travelling is happiness and also disappointment. She opens her eyes and counts the lights on the highway. When she gets to a hundred, she starts again. They enter the bus terminal and she's already done this ten times.

"I'm serious, I can't buy you anything," Marta says again.

Between the taxi and their bus fares and what's going to be a long night, they'll have spent 5,000 pesos; 25,000 will be left. They walk to the platform. How long will their money last? They'll have to get settled, find a school that will accept Evelyn for three weeks. Or a month. Not much longer. Marta gets angry at Hugo's voice telling her not to keep so much money in the bank. When you need it you don't have it, he says. What if he withdraws it all?

She doesn't finish doing the maths. The television is on in the station's waiting room and her gaze falls on the screen. People are crowded around it. She suddenly realizes Hugo isn't using his phone. Without taking her eyes off the image on the television, Marta reaches for her daughter's hand.

"Why don't we go to the convenience store?"

MYJESUS, during present dangers, cover us withyour-preciousblood. This part is supposed to go at the beginning but Mónica's nervous, she's lost her place and is reciting the prayer out of order. Marta asks if she's heard about the train, the one that crashed in Haedo, and this angers her—she doesn't care about the news right now. She wants to know what happened and wishes Marta would tell her without her having to ask.

People get their hopes up on a mega jackpot night. Mónica's feeling a little hopeful herself, which always happens when the girls come to Colón. She makes all sorts of plans and in the end none of them happen because all Marta wants to do is go to the river and sleep. Not long after they arrive, Mónica's desperate for them to leave. But the hope returns every time they plan a visit. It makes her restless. She badly wants to give up her rituals, is afraid their mother will come too and at the same time, dreams of the summer together, of getting Marta temporary work at the casino, giving her a few sex-toy clients. She's got more and more of them, women are very unsatisfied. Mónica feels strong but also a bit silly about hoping this will happen every time her older sister comes to visit. It doesn't matter how much

Mónica helps her, Marta won't acknowledge any of it. And at the end of the night, people will have lost more money than ever.

It's better not to know anything about the train crash yet, Jesus's wounds are enough for the time being. But Marta sends her another message. She won't let the subject go:

I think Hugo was on the train.

"GOAL FOR TIGRE, mate," a firefighter sergeant lies into the air, into the darkness, into the silence on the other side of the window.

With a flashlight, he searches for the voice he's just heard and the location of his new friend. Every section of the carriage that he lights up is a jumble of navy blue, dirty white, dark green, grey, brown. The people all look the same, their clothes, their colours. He can't tell where one ends and the other begins. They're stuck together, welded to one another. It's only pieces, frayed human parts, that poke out of windows like torn bin bags. His boss shouts for help, to get a body out, to start somewhere. A voice in the human haystack asks him how the game's going. It's louder than the other voices begging to be taken out and the hands that dig their nails into him when he passes by with the flashlight.

The firefighters look for the end of the ball of yarn: someone they can remove whole through the window to begin the rescue from the wreck of a carriage that crashed into a train stopped at Haedo Station.

"No way, I'm a Tigre fan too." This time the sergeant's not lying as he chats with the passenger in an attempt at maintaining the man's sanity, and his own while he's at it, because what he sees is causing his mind to play tricks on him—the blue faces, the bulging eyes, the bloody teeth. The man has stopped answering. Some cries get louder while others go out like a hellfire of cicadas burning in the sun.

The sergeant moves the beam of his flashlight from left to right, up and down. He's getting used to the jumble of humans in the dark, is able to distinguish one body from the next. They've fallen in a row. He reckons the passenger's head is on top of the avalanche.

"Goal for Tigre, mate," he says a little louder, in a voice he wants to sound strong, calm, confident, heroic and paternal, but which is that of a sergeant from the Haedo Fire Department.

"Whose goal was it?"

The sergeant hears this from somewhere at the back. "El Chino, who'd you think it was gonna be, guy. Where are you?"

"Over here."

At the edge of the circle of light, a hand. A hand and a holy card. It's all very dark, but the sergeant recognizes the image.

"You brought St Expeditus? Don't let him go."

"Am I going to die?"

I'm an idiot, the sergeant says to himself. His mind continues to race towards lateral thinking, free association, escape. Everything he sees is like a cartoon: the bulging eyes, the busted hands. It's like when the Pink Panther is squashed by an elephant, or an anvil falls on him, or his neck is wrung.

The sergeant moves the flashlight more slowly, trying to locate the Tigre fan's face, until he finds it. It's not blue yet. The man can still be saved.

"We're almost there," he promises, lying for the second time that night.

The other firefighters try to break the wall of the carriage that's like a can of sardines. It's impossible to pull a body out without handling it like a rag. At this point they're all wondering whether it would be better to remove the dead from the carriage, as if they were pieces of metal, even though doing so would create a scene of carnage. It already is one after all. The rescue continues to be delayed, those who are still alive won't make it. The firefighters talk to the man sticking out beyond the others like a figurehead. They tell him to hold on, throw oil on him from a jug someone bought at the supermarket. The cries are unbearable.

The sergeant tosses bottles of water to those at the back. One person is laughing at the madness of it all. The Tigre fan is also smiling. He has long hair and a bit of a Jesus beard. He's a lot thinner than the dead body toppling onto him. The fire chief appears through the roof of the carriage with a man who looks to be the head of operations.

"Get the cutter, we're gonna put a hole in this," they yell. "We'll pull them out from above."

The sergeant turns around but then he changes his mind and yells through the window.

"I'll be right back," he says. "Wait for me here."

"It's bad, isn't it? Am I going to die?" the Tigre fan asks again.

But the firefighter sergeant doesn't answer and Hugo is once more left in the solitude, anguish and pitch dark of the carriage.

THERE'S NO such thing as chance. It's divine justice. Good luck is a lie. Mónica knows this as "slot manager", her position, in English, at the Colón Casino. She goes over the words of the holy wounds rosary one by one. Salvation doesn't come free. Someone has to suffer the wounds. God doesn't save you just like that, because salvation isn't social planning. Jesus died on the cross. I offer you the wounds ofourlordje-suschrist to heal the wounds of our souls. It's crystal clear. It's not a matter of repeating it and that's that, you need to understand the text. Mónica says the rosary conscientiously. Every word of it. And it works just as it should. It works.

To heal your soul, someone else needs to suffer. That's what it means. It's a metaphor. Someone gets screwed over so that you're saved. Life's like that. But not just anyone gets screwed over and not just anyone is saved, that's the thing. Marta wrote:

I think Hugo was on the train

Sometimes that's what God's like, literal. Not metaphorical.

Mónica doesn't know how to respond. She thinks for a few seconds.

You don't say.

✓✓

I offer you the wounds ofourlordjesuschrist to heal the
wounds of our souls. She's repeated the word wounds so
many times she begins to feel pain. It's an undefined pain
in some part of her body. On a mega jackpot night, no one
thinks about the pain to come. Mónica stops walking through
the main hall, her gaze lost on one of the Ramses, on his
muscles and treasure, which flashes on and off, announcing
a prize. Salvation is something else. She wants to tell Marta
one more thing.

We'll be fine tomorrow.

✓✓

H UGO HEARS NOISES above his head. They're louder than the shouts. This is how it's going to end, he thinks, something is going to come down onto me and squash me. But ahead of the panic comes a thin and powerful ray of light that descends onto Expeditus and lowers along his arm, which is still raised. Hugo feels illuminated, understands he's at the tip of the mountain. The light coming from the heavens is eclipsed by the silhouette of a head with a helmet. It's not a God, a Christ or a saint, it's not divine justice labelling him guilty and condemning him to a miserable death. It's the Haedo fire chief.

"We're gonna get you out of here," the man tells him.

Hugo thinks quickly. He considers possible outcomes: death, injury, jail, flight. Then combinations of these four possibilities: go to jail paralysed, flee in a wheelchair, take off running as soon as they put him down on the platform. While all of this is going through his head, the firefighters lift him up by his armpits and pull. It's like he's going to be split in two. He's trapped between dead bodies that won't let him free. With all of his being, even the tips of his hairs, he pushes up. Afterwards, he won't remember whether he cried out. Though he will recall the moment the bodies gave

34

way, his bare foot stepping on something, a hand grabbing hold of his ankle, wanting to bury him again, and the kick he gave that freed him. The firefighters slip Hugo through a hole he wouldn't have thought was large enough for a leg. He's born again, and it's just like the first time, forty-three years prior: through an impossibly small hole while two blokes in uniform pull on his arms from outside of it, with no grace or love. He focuses on what's important. He's got his legs. What he doesn't have are his trousers.

Hugo is still on the roof of the carriage when they strap him into a stretcher and put a neck brace on him. The second he understands that fleeing is impossible, he lets go of his mobile. With what remains of his consciousness, he hears it ricochet somewhere. His ID cards are in his bag, somewhere inside the carriage. Hugo is nobody. I dodged a bullet, he thinks, and they lower him onto the platform.

"My apologies, mate, I lied. We lost three nothing."

The sergeant and Tigre fan is one of the men carrying the stretcher. "I'm Marcelo, you're going to be fine, they're taking you to the hospital. What's your name?"

Hugo stares at Marcelo and keeps his mouth closed. He opens the fist with St Expeditus in it. Marcelo understands what he wants and takes the wrinkled holy card, moved.

E VERYTHING MOVES quickly now. Domínguez crosses the concentric circles around the disaster. Neighbours, journalists, ambulances and people looking for family members run in the opposite direction, towards the hospitals. Then he crosses the tape, the police, the rescue workers vomiting, throwing water onto themselves before submerging in the dark again. Fifty metres away, his car beams light up the throng of helmets and metal.

The detective avoids the handrails on the stretchers as he walks along the platform. He shows his ID to a couple of officers who block his way and then let him pass. He loves doing this.

From afar, he can make out the silhouette of one carriage inside another. But from up close it's a cave. The firefighters remove bodies and lay them on the cement floor. All of them are dead. Some of them are pieces of the dead. The firefighters place them there carefully, they're not used to so many cadavers. Forensics shows less etiquette when they put the bodies in black bags and lay them on the last stretch of the platform. Before all the bodies are taken away, Domínguez counts them. It's an obsession of his. The bodies are mixed up with other things that aren't human. Backpacks, sneakers, bags. A bike.

In the grey mountain of inanimate objects, something lights up. The screen of a mobile phone. Domínguez reads it quickly. It's a message. A question:

You there?

It's from Marta. One of the thousands of possible Martas. There's no such thing as chance, he says to himself—it's his catchphrase—and he does one of the things that led to him being known on the force as Domínguez the madman. As an unimpeachable detective with a good record. He bends down and picks up the device. I shouldn't be doing this, he thinks, but he touches the screen to read the message. It's not blocked. He opens the conversation:

Come home it's urgent
The police are looking for you
Where are you

Sorry, I fucked up.
✓✓

It's not chance, it's a coincidence. I shouldn't be doing this, Domínguez thinks again, but he doesn't think about what comes next. He types a response to Marta's question:

You there?

                                                          Yes.
                                                           ✓✓

He presses send and puts his discovery in the right pocket
of his trousers.

T HE YELLOW COACH parks in front of the platform and Evelyn's stomach ache disappears. It's a double-decker bus, the same one they take every summer. But she's twice as excited this time, because it feels more like an escape than a vacation at her aunt's. Evelyn's mum is always saying her stomach aches are selective, and she doesn't like it because they really hurt. She chooses the window seat and reclines, as though this way she'll only see the sky. It's what she imagines flying in a plane is like. When the bus accelerates, the feeling of vertigo causes her stomach to tighten, just like on a rollercoaster.

Gastric sensations are the code Evelyn uses to talk to Marta. It's a way to avoid being hounded with questions like how are you feeling, what's wrong, why won't you tell me, what are you thinking, what's going on with you. They thus resolve their tacit disagreement with digestion metaphors, thereby avoiding words and pacifying anxieties. Evelyn is now thirteen. If Marta can't learn to handle her daughter being a mystery, she's going to lose her forever.

"It's just gas, don't worry."

Marta eases Evelyn's body onto her lap and covers her daughter with her jacket. With her left hand, she plays with Evelyn's hair, and with her right, she checks her mobile.

When she finds her most recent chat with Olga, she types, "Don't worry." She erases this message and types, "Gone for a few days." Then she erases this too.

Mónica, on the other hand, is sending non-stop messages.

> Have you eaten?
> What does Evelyn have for breakfast?
> Careful your mobile doesn't connect to Uruguay's network on the highway, it'll cost you a fortune

Nothing from Hugo. He's not getting in touch. Marta looks at the screen every two or three minutes. The bus is already on the highway headed north. The speed at which the trees, houses, billboards, shadows are left behind results in the mirage that Marta experiences when she travels: the kilometres seem to be days. But they're not. A message from Hugo:

> Yes.

Marta waits for him to say something else. Yes, I'm alive? Yes, I've been arrested? Yes, I'm on my way? Yes, I'm hurt, get me a lawyer, put Evelyn on, make roast chicken with potatoes? Yes, I love you, save yourself, go screw yourself? Yes what? She puts the phone away. Hugo has been an abyss for some time now.

The air conditioning on the bus is freezing her fingers. She has to go to the toilet but holds it so Evelyn can stay where she is. There's pleasure for her in the melancholic feeling of being in transit, an ideal state, even on a night like this. She wishes the trip were much longer. It doesn't bother her that a few strangers can hear the sounds she makes when she goes to the toilet and can watch her sleep. The forced intimacy with the other passengers is less uncomfortable than the physical obligations of familiarity, of two people imposing proximity on one another, spending time together, talking every day, sharing a room when they have nothing to say. Everyone's asleep, except for the guy sweet-talking somebody in a hushed voice on his mobile a few seats back, and the woman up front, who sticks her rear end in the face of the twenty-something next to her, giving him no time to bend his legs towards the aisle so she can get by, stumbling, en route to the loo with a roll of toilet paper in her hand. Marta follows the woman, startling her daughter when she manoeuvres into the aisle.

"Get some rest, I'll wake you up when we're at the bridges," she promises.

So Evelyn pretends to sleep.

Marta isn't overwhelmed. She no longer needs to organize her thoughts—everything is coming to her in a logical sequence. And she's not worried. On the contrary. Denouements are a form of relief.

When she returns from the toilet, she has five messages from Mónica:

Don't let these problems get the best of you. There's a way forwards.

I know you need help and solace.

Repeat this prayer three times and share it with ten friends who need the same thing you do.

Don't break the chain.

I offer you the wounds of Our Lord Jesus Christ...

Sixth message from Mónica:

Are you in Zárate yet? I'm sending you the rosary of the holy wounds.

Marta types:

Ok

✓✓

Against the backdrop of the night, the bridge's lights stand out like a Christmas tree. Soon they'll be in Paraná de las Palmas and Marta will once again feel that crossing the river is a promise. It's been this way since New Year's 1987. After the toast, Marta and Mónica got into their parents' white Renault 12 that was headed for Brazil. As they crossed the bridge, the girls rolled down the windows and breathed the air that seemed warm and strange and thick. Mónica said that she wanted to live in a place like that and Marta said she was such an idiot because they weren't even at the border. Then they had fruit cake and slept for hours. Their father drove more than a thousand kilometres and they arrived at a resort town that looked a lot like Santa Teresita in Argentina. But everything was still exotic, fascinating and sad.

It's the only thing she and Mónica have to remember. Whenever they spend time together, they go over the same stories. They'd made friends with three Argentinian guys, each hoping to find herself a boyfriend. The guys had pressured them into stealing a few packs of gum, little colourful sticks, at the supermarket, and to sneaking into the pool at an upscale hotel, but nothing came of it. The guest house they'd stayed at was big and old, the walls a faded pink and the roof tiles broken. In the dining room, there was unfamiliar fruit and a host who organized a dance contest every night. Marta was forced to participate as the family representative. She won the hula-hoop contest and the prize was T-shirts with a picture of the peak of Pão de Açúcar and their names printed on them. Marta still uses hers at night, and also the sheets her parents bought in the centre of Capão da Canoa the day they left. They drove home in the Renault 12, having been in the water just once, with many-coloured Salvador do Bomfin ribbons around their wrists. People in their neighbourhood said the family had been to Brazil and provided no further details. The next summer their father wasn't with them any more and their mother didn't know how to drive. In the memories Marta has invented, she's floating in the sea.

Now she feels the water's proximity and tears up. A little. Silently. A couple of tears. It's not exactly crying. It's the slightest overflow of a subterranean river that touches the surface and drains a bit of its torrent, as though doing so will allow it to return to its course and continue to flow below ground, burying in its depths the only question Marta asks herself from time to time, which falls short of taking the shape of words and closely resembles a reproach. She searches among her feelings but can't determine whether the malaise is Hugo or her past. She wipes the moment and the tears away with her hand. It doesn't matter.

Alexithymia. Difficulty getting in touch with your emotions. That's the last thing she learnt in psychology before she dropped out of university. When her father died, not one of them cried. This difficulty with emotions doesn't seem problematic to her. All things considered, it's a virtue. A superpower that protects her from all but one thing: the possibility of her daughter inheriting the gift. Marta doesn't want to be a stomach ache. The thought that Evelyn feels nothing for her is terrifying.

They're on the bridge now and Evelyn makes an effort to keep her eyes closed. She enjoys the moment. When she and Marta are sad, it's like they love each other more. A bright light illuminates her face and she can't bear not to look. Marta combs her daughter's hair with her fingers. Outside, the cables pass in front of Evelyn's eyes like a hypnotist's pendulum.

"Mum, the police…"

"Go to sleep already, Evelyn."

FORTY-THREE DEAD. Domínguez is in the passenger seat because Ramírez is always first to the pickup. And when Domínguez isn't driving, he can't focus on his mental calculations. Until today, he had 510 stiffs. In exactly three decades of service, that's seventeen per year. One every twenty days. It's a large number, but if all of a sudden there are forty-three more, it could change your record. Give the impression of something it's not. The detective finds himself in a dilemma: Should he add today's cadavers to his count? If the question is how many dead he's seen in his life, then yes. But not all of them are his.

They leave Haedo Station slowly. Ramírez is driving because he got behind the wheel while he was waiting for Domínguez. He never left the pickup. Five minutes in the Toyota and it already seems a night like any other. In a couple of bars, people are watching what happened a few blocks away on television. It doesn't really make much sense for him to go on counting stiffs. It's not impressive nowadays: anyone can see pictures of cadavers on WhatsApp before forensics does. Anyone can see a hundred stiffs a year—if they want to. In the homicide unit they're counted one at a time, two at a time. A triple murder happens once in a lifetime. Today Domínguez saw all the bodies that accumulate over two-and-a-half years in one go.

It's better he doesn't ask why Ramírez stayed in the pickup at the station and why the hell he gets behind the wheel whenever he has the chance. 510 plus 43 equals 553. That's a big difference, but the average over thirty years is more or less the same: one every twenty days. Seen this way, today's count won't change his record much. Domínguez hopes the mobile he removed from the platform doesn't start ringing next to his balls before they drop the Toyota off and he leaves the new guy. He doesn't know him well yet. Ramírez is too quiet. So is the mobile.

Now what needs to be determined is whether one of the forty-three is Hugo Víctor Lamadrid, primary suspect in the homicide of Carlos David Cristaldo, Paraguayan, nineteen years old, found in Las Catonas creek, near the industrial park, inside a bag with the Barça crest on it, a bag capable of holding a skinny corpse more or less comfortably. This description caused Marta to go pale, though she maintained her composure and silence as best she could, like any wife would, whether out of shock, fright or collusion. What Domínguez doesn't feel appropriate for any wife is the fact that Marta took more than two hours just to send a short message to her husband, to see if he was okay. Maybe they're not very close as a couple.

In a way he can't explain, and that will eventually be even more incomprehensible for the department head, Domínguez knows that this phone belongs to the Hugo he's looking for and that this Marta is the stick-thin but still pretty foxy lady he met earlier that evening. Why he decides to risk screwing up his life, his not-so-distant retirement, his homicide clearance rate—the best in the suburbs at 459 cases solved out of a total of 510—with wrongful procedure and removal of evidence is also beyond explanation. Domínguez has one of his world-famous hunches.

It's not just a train that derailed tonight. Of this he's certain, but he's not able to formulate a hypothesis for his disquiet. Because Ramírez is presumptuous, he gets behind the wheel whenever he can. And if Domínguez isn't driving, he can't think clearly.

T HE ROULETTE PLAYERS are a different breed. They're gentlemen. After their last ball has been played, they leave without a fuss. Or they stay and drink whisky. They say good evening, dress well. Though she knows them all, Mónica greets them as though they were tourists and wishes them a pleasant stay in the City of Colón. She's friendly but distant. Let them do as they please with their lives. The blackjack players are different too. Except for the Chinese men. They play with a lot of money and are loyal clients, but they don't have manners and drink too much. They don't seem to be friends, and don't talk to each other—that is, unless they're shouting or barely whispering. They sound angry. Mónica gathers these men are part of a mafia, so when they're at the casino, she comes and goes through the room without taking her eyes off their hands, always alert in case one of them takes out a revolver and starts to fire.

They're not at the casino today, but Mónica is feeling as anxious as she does when they are. Though she never eats at work, she goes over to the bar. She pushes the rosary towards the bottom of the shallow pocket on her maroon waistcoat with its black tuxedo neck. Her tube skirt prevents her from climbing onto one of the high bar stools. At least hers doesn't have a slit up to her left thigh like the other women's. Management takes this kind of thing into consideration with Mónica, a sign she'll soon have a better position, a senior one.

Her hips against the counter, she chews on a white-bread sandwich and scans the main hall. She locates the blonde and decides to begin with her. Mónica doesn't know her name but she does know the woman works for the municipality and that the colour of her hair is artificial. Mónica also knows that she's going to make a scene, like she always does. Whenever she's at the casino, the bleached blonde threatens to file a big-money lawsuit, a class action for the slot machine scam. They're programmed so people lose at four in the morning, she says. She has the proof, she yells.

"Ma'am, we're closing the main hall."

"When I file a lawsuit against the casino, you'll be without work, Mónica."

"Don't forget that Thursday is ladies' night and you'll enjoy two for one if you dine with your girlfriends. We accept all cards."

The blonde fixes her eyes on the little machine, which spits chips out at her, and plays another round.

"Today you leave on time," Mónica says under her breath, and continues to make her way through the casino, asking the gentlemen to wrap up and the women to come back on Thursday with their girlfriends, when two dine for one and there's a full menu with dessert and coffee, international cuisine. Half an hour like this, courteous but firm, somewhere between friendly, which is part of the trade, and moral superiority, herding weak souls towards the exit. The day's drunk goes at the Double Dragon machine again. "It swallowed the chip," he yells. "Thieves." There goes the blonde with her card. She approaches and offers to file a lawsuit against the casino. As she always does. Mónica requests a company taxi to take her to the bus terminal later.

She walks the ten blocks to her house. The night is foggy in anticipation of summer but Mónica is cold. She has a bit of time to get everything in order before dawn. She drinks a cup of rose-hip tea, makes a mental list of her priorities and decides on the first step. She puts the contents of one of her two night-table drawers in a box decorated with drawings of butterflies and French words. In it go the imitation jade Chinese balls, the little bottle of strawberry oil with champagne, the baby egg, the waterproof golden duck, an unopened tube of anal lubricant, the bubblegum pink feathers, the sparkly mask and several vibrators, among them the realistic Double 30 as yet unused. That it's realistic is what least excites Mónica. The box in her hand, she stands there thinking, unsure where to put it. In the end, she decides to push it under the bed, but she leaves out the Pearl 2000 with clitoral stimulator.

While she fills the bathtub she changes her mind. She's not really in the mood for the Pearl 2000 with clitoral stimulator. Because she feels like crying and doesn't desire anything that resembles a man, not even a man with a clitoral stimulator. The best thing would be to climax quickly, nothing else. Seated on her bed, she can't make up her mind. Marta is still 200 kilometres away, but Mónica can already feel the effect her sister has on her. That unease. Marta will be arriving in two hours, but it's like she's already there. Mónica decides it would be better to take advantage of the moment. It could be her last chance in a long time.

She gets a little aroused, thinking about the urgency of the situation, so she places a small red handkerchief over the lamp on her night table and searches for a memory of similar lighting. She finds it in the hallway of a casino hotel in Las Vegas. This she does while twisting her nipple under the tuxedo neck of her waistcoat. She kneels down on the floor and with her other hand reaches under her skirt. But she has to stop because if she rips her corporate uniform, they'll deduct it from her salary.

"I'm an idiot, an idiot," she repeats.

She grabs hold of the thread of excitement she feels. Tries to cling to someone. An idea without a face. It's the idea that's important. No one in particular. The Chinese man with the black shirt appears. The more she tries to avoid thinking about some things, the worse. In a mammoth effort to stay aroused, on her knees, her hands gripping the edge of the bed, she opts for the realistic Double 30 with gel applied. Mónica is not lacking for will and she bends it into a horseshoe, positions each of its ends in an orifice and lets out a moan. She doesn't like to hear herself so she waits a little, closes her eyes, moves her waist and continues in silence.

It looks to her like it measures thirty centimetres, but she does not approve of it being called realistic. There is nothing in real life that works the way it does. It goes in and out well, could be called ergonomic, friendly, something to that effect. Realism is overrated. She tries to focus on an Italian singer in an attempt at forgetting the Chinese man. A singer she loves. She can't remember his name. Nor can she keep moving her arm because after a while it starts to hurt a lot. What she has to do is keep her hand still and move her hips, only she's not into that. She starts to feel uncomfortable and ridiculous with so pretentious a toy.

Remembering the Italian singer's name proves impossible. He was blind and very romantic, and he had a beautiful voice. The thought that he can't see Mónica gets her excited again. Imagining herself with a blind man and getting aroused in this new and different way was just what she was after tonight. From now on she won't be fantasizing about anyone who can see her. She writhes against the realistic Double 30. It's too bad she doesn't have the Pearl with clitoral stimulator in reach now because her hand is cramping and her knees hurt against the cold tiles and the fantasies are piling up, cancelling each other out, until they fade first into nothing and then into thoughts and questions about what could have happened to Marta and Evelyn, and what everything is going to be like now, with the three of them there.

I T'S THE SAME WALL. The paint grey or green or sky
blue, like the memory of a colour. Hugo knows where
he is when he opens his eyes. Even before he does, because
when he wakes up, he's shaken by a familiar light and the
sound of voices that are echoes from another dimension
where people live and talk and laugh. The wall is closing in
on him, its pores open wide, and as he feels it coming down
onto him, he tries to escape by looking away. He turns his
head and it's like falling back into a pit. Everything is moving
and then the image comes into focus again. It's a corridor.
He's sure of it: it's the same corridor where Evelyn spent a
night. On an identical stretcher, against this wall that's not
grey or green or sky blue, with an IV and oxygen until it
was day outside.

Hugo swore to the wall that they would never see each
other again. Evelyn was already breathing fine, but the doctors weren't ready to release her from the hospital. Hugo and
Marta were so scared they said yes to everything and stood
in that corridor all night. That's why Hugo remembers it
all perfectly—the wall, the corridor that's not green or sky
blue or grey. He remembers the wall perfectly, as he does
Evelyn, her eyes rolling, not responding, her body so stiff it

was as though the water in the shower didn't wet her, and he remembers his fear of breaking her. His hands tremble at the memory. Marta shouted, "Get her out, Hugo, get her out," and didn't understand that if he held Evelyn too tightly, she might break. That tiny body of hers, it was so easy to break.

You really have to be careful because there are bodies that don't let you know, they don't crack, don't bleed, don't shout. Marta has no idea how easy it is for someone to break on you from one second to the next. Hugo knows this all too well. The faded grey green sky-blue paint reminds him of everything he knows now, and he knows a lot more than he did that night, all of which he spent talking to the wall, begging it not to let anything happen to Evelyn, while Marta blamed him for not having taken the water heater out of the bathroom. "You almost killed your daughter," she said. Later on she too would turn into a faded wall that wasn't grey or sky blue or green.

What a son of a bitch St Expeditus is, looking for Hugo on the train, waiting until he's seen the man has fallen to say to him: This is what you get, for what you did, now you see what it looks like from down below, interred in a pit with pieces of people and metal and shoes and things that don't belong to anyone, buried, among cracking bones and bulging eyes, the air disappearing. You're jumbled up with others. Like scrap metal. Mixed in. Damaged. It's what you deserve.

His cranium weighs a tonne, moving his head is like loosening a rusty screw. Without raising it, he turns to see another body lying on his left. Along the corridor there are two rows of stretchers. Hugo plans his next move with the facts he has on hand. He's still in Haedo, the tragedy hasn't taken him very far. He's alone in the hospital emergency room with others who have been abandoned just like him. Using his hands and elbows, he props his torso up a little so he can see better. There are no doctors or nurses in sight. They're attending urgent cases. The pain in the back of his neck clouds his judgement. St Expeditus, patron of urgent matters, sonofafucking bitch. He moves his body slowly until he's sitting up, his thin, bare legs hanging from the stretcher. He holds on to the edge and tries to move his bruised feet. From waist up, he's in pretty good shape—he's still got his briefs and shirt on. They put the neck brace on over his long hair. No one is looking at him. Some people are sleeping and others are complaining.

This must be the corridor for those who are better off. But how to be sure? You can be completely damaged on the inside and not feel a thing. Pain isn't always proportional to harm. You could leave through the door on foot and die on the next block. Or the next day. You could have a blood clot travelling through your body. Or wandering around in your brain until suddenly you can't walk or forget your name. When Beto crashed his motorcycle, Pamela bounced back up like a spring and took off running down the highway, and it turned out all of her was broken. That your body lets you know—that's bullshit. It's not always like that. If our bodies let us know, things wouldn't go wrong.

Which is why Hugo decides to get up and take off running. To see what happens. He removes the neck brace, touches his vertebra, moves his head slowly. Now the kid on the next stretcher is looking at him. His situation is the opposite of Hugo's: he's got his trousers on and his torso is bare. His shoulder is a little cut up and his arm is violet. Hugo reckons they're in the corridor for those without hope. He talks to the kid, attempts to avert his eyes from the body part that's frightening.

"Hey, mate, can I ask you a favour? Look at me. How do I look to you? My head, my face? Am I bleeding? What about the back of me, everything in order? Don't look at yourself, look at me."

There's panic in the kid's eyes. He can't feel his arm, he says.

"Your shoulder's a little hurt. Don't move, you don't want to dislocate anything."

Hugo gets down off the stretcher and touches the floor with his bare feet. They hurt, but the cold tiles feel good. He talks very softly to his neighbour in the corridor, who begins to cry, to plead.

"Don't shout, mate, don't cry, don't be a wimp. You're not that bad off. Know what? Lend me your trousers. I'll get dressed and go find a doctor to help you right away."

He keeps an eye on the corridor and unbuttons his neighbour's fly, lowers the zip slowly and trying not to brush the kid's balls, raises his body slightly to slide his jeans over his hips. The kid cries out as Hugo pulls off one leg, then the

56

other. He balances between the two stretchers while he gets his legs into the borrowed trousers and tucks his half-ripped shirt, which is stained with blood, sweat and dirt, into his waist. Hugo doesn't like to wear his shirts hanging out.

"The fit's perfect, mate. I'll tell them to come look for you. What's your name?"

The reply comes softly, between sobs. Hugo moves his ear up to the kid's mouth.

"Do you have a girlfriend, Alejo?… What's her name?… I'm going to leave through the door now and look for Andrea. I'll tell the doctor to help you. Don't cry. Breathe deeply. Inhale, exhale. Look at me."

Hugo is talking loudly now, accompanying his words with a movement of his hands, up and down, from his diaphragm to his nose and back to his diaphragm, like the conductor of an orchestra who can't decide whether to begin the symphony.

"Inhale, exhale, inhale, exhale. It'll do you good. I'm leaving now. Inhale, that's it, breathe deeply. Exhale, easy does it."

Hugo walks backwards slowly while he shows Alejo how to breathe. The kid stops him, asks for his name.

"Don't worry about me… Expeditus. St Expeditus is my name."

D OMÍNGUEZ'S OFFICE opens onto a French balcony
and it's the only one on the first floor with the green
shutters closed. Ramírez has tried repeatedly to leave the
window open and on one occasion, almost managed to
place a potted tree on the balcony. It's another silent war
they fight. There's a lot of commotion on the ground floor
for a Tuesday, but the Morón Department Head hasn't
arrived yet. They'll have to wait and see if he's heard
about the train—that is, if he didn't fall asleep watching
the Argentinian version of *Strictly Come Dancing*. Domínguez
hurries to finish his report before it's daylight out and the
wood floors in all the offices creak under the department
head's dress shoes, and he begins to mess with the detective in that way of his that's like butting him with a gun.
Mancuso doesn't put pressure on him like the previous
heads, but treats him as though he were harmless. A has-
been. From the nineties, when the situation was bad. Like
a mastermind. An eccentric.

Domínguez hits the keyboard hard, dictating to himself
in a whisper. He writes:

The undersigned, Detective Commissioner Osvaldo Marcial Domínguez, reports his actions at 21:10 yesterday when he appeared at the residence of Hugo Víctor Lamadrid, located in blah blah blah

Thin rays of light begin to filter through the shutters. Like Ramírez, Mancuso is always hounding him to open the window, to enjoy the view and the privilege of having an office at the front of the rundown mansion where they work. That is until a building goes up and the neighbours have no trouble seeing Domínguez struggle to draft a report. The facts are few and they're very clear, but they refuse to organize themselves into sentences and paragraphs. Domínguez is sweating. He drinks straight from a two-litre bottle of Coke he found on someone's desk. It's already warm and has no fizz. He lashes out against bureaucracy like an insecure student on a written exam. His prose is awful and it irritates him, though nobody cares.

Mrs Marta Lacase, who introduces herself as the cohabiting partner of Hugo Víctor Lamadrid, declares she is unaware of the facts about which she is being interrogated and the whereabouts of the suspect and adds that the aforementioned Lamadrid provides a locksmith service and left his home to attend to an urgent situation that, according to the declarant… the declarant declares…

The verb confuses Domínguez, he needs a bite of something sweet. There's a good selection of no-name-brand items in the vending machine down the hall. In his head, he goes over what he should and shouldn't report in writing, as well as a story arc that connects obligatory procedures and intuitive actions.

…considering the temporal coincidence between the railway accident and the suspect going to Once to offer a locksmith service… the undersigned went to Haedo Station in order to conduct an on-site investigation and verify or rule out the hypothesis that…

No. The mere mention of the word hypothesis and he's liable to be warned and even sanctioned with a shot to the testicles from a regulation firearm. He looks for an elegant solution that doesn't mention intuition or hypotheses. Whenever Mancuso hears these terms, his hand reaches for his regulation Bersa. It's a reflex action, an impulse. Domínguez is also impulsive, but his instincts differ from Mancuso's: the latter covers his arse while the former puts it at risk. For example, by removing one of the latest models of a Samsung mobile phone, which is very likely to be the property of Hugo Víctor Lamadrid, from the scene of the accident, and placing it in the bottom of his right trouser pocket, actions that his boss, the department head, will understand have been omitted from the present report.

It's now daylight out and there's not much to tell Mancuso. The incursion into the Don Guido pizzeria to watch the round-up of the day's matches on television: no. The official list of the dead and wounded made known at 4:45 a.m. and the news that Lamadrid isn't on it: yes. Despite the record that has earned him prestige on the force, Domínguez officially begins the day as a useless member who doesn't have a damn clue where his suspect went. Unofficially, the situation is getting worse. Another thing the document won't mention is the friendly visit Domínguez paid to forensics, where El Gordo Mario thanked him for the coffee and *alfajor* cookie, and informed him of the remains of two middle-aged John Does as yet unidentified.

Domínguez has been rocking in his broken chair for years. He has to make an effort to hold himself upright in front of the computer and this messes with his sciatic nerve. Writing reports is tiring. If it takes them that long to change his damn chair, who knows when they'll have the DNA of some remains no one cares about. The bodies haven't been claimed by family members. Those who have been to the hospital and the morgue found the wounded or dead person they were looking for. No one's looking for these two and all Domínguez has to go on is the impersonal and non-transferable certainty that one of them is Hugo Víctor Lamadrid. Marta Lacase and his other relatives and friends have not been particularly active in searching for him, and even less so in reporting his disappearance, which is entirely logical given the circumstances.

But Domínguez doesn't buy the logic. The most obvious response is surely not the right one. If Ángela had been in Marta's place, what would she have done? She wouldn't necessarily have run desperately to the emergency room at Posadas. Or forced herself to withstand the desperation in order to leave the possibility for flight open. Wives behave in more sophisticated ways than police hypotheses.

Using his ex as an example of casuistry in a report for the department head isn't a good idea either. What a foul mood he's in. Now he has to return to the house in Ituzaingó and find a simple answer that will pacify Mancuso, even though he, Domínguez, doesn't have the slightest idea what's going on. He has the best homicide clearance rate in the suburbs, but human relations are a mystery that eludes him.

PART TWO

M ARINA IS TALKING into the mirror. She tells it the transport minister might call and that there are a couple of family members at the door to the morgue, waiting for the programme to begin. The mirror asks her which family members.

"A mother and a husband," she says.

"They can't find the bodies?" Sandra's image cross-questions her producer.

"The bodies have been found, they've all been identified."

"So then?"

Sandra Lagos has stopped talking to Marina in the mirror. She's turned around to face her. One of her eyes is made up, the other isn't. Marina doesn't know which one to talk to. She focuses on the eye that's finished, as it seems friendlier, and explains that the family members have been convinced to wait a little longer so that they can be on air.

"How could you have asked them to wait? That's not the way I treat people. Bring them in to the studio, get them some coffee. They'll be more comfortable indoors in this heat. Poor people."

Sandra Lagos says all this while looking at Marina in the mirror again. They're now applying make-up to her other eye. If Marina asks Sandra about the minister, she won't answer. Sandra doesn't like to have civil servants on her programme. She prefers to speak to the people.

El Rifle is complaining to Marina over WhatsApp. His evening programme was on when the accident happened. They left "the rifle" with a block of guests there for something else and went to the production truck. He was on air for eighteen minutes—that's it. El Rifle tracks this on his phone's stopwatch. Now he's desperate for information:

Have you heard anything else?

Marina doesn't answer. What a tough morning, it's like a million things are happening, but nothing is. The director asks her what time the family members will be there, and now everyone assumes they're coming and Marina hasn't called them back yet. El Rifle is still bugging her on WhatsApp:

Can you get a firefighter?

"WE'RE GOING to have to do something, Marta."

Mónica swats at a fly with a dish towel right in front of her sister's face, to rouse her. But Marta is suspended in the moment, she sees no future or past. They're drinking *mate* in the kitchen with the television on mute. Evelyn has been told to go shower and unpack her things in the room Mónica calls "the study" because there's a desk in it, and also because it's where she keeps her direct-sale products and the pull-out couch sprinkled with pink pillows in the shapes of lips and hearts, which she asks her clients to take a seat on. Evelyn comes and goes along the hallway and the sisters chat in fits and starts.

Mónica checks the news on her laptop.

"Marta, he's not in the paper."

"What's that?"

"Hugo. There's a list of the dead and he's not on it."

"Well, he will be."

"No, Marta. They say here that these are all the dead people, that there are no more bodies."

"Then I'll give him a call later and ask him where he is."

"Are you out of your mind? What about Evelyn? What are you going to tell her?"

"That he died."

"And does Hugo know?"

"What that he died? I don't believe he does. He sent me a message. I didn't say anything to Evelyn."

"Or to me."

"It's that I thought you'd gotten your hopes up."

EVELYN IS UNABLE to react, standing in the middle of her three-by-two-metre hiding spot with a window facing the street. The few items of clothing she brought are already folded on a shelf in the closet. The picture of Romeo is stuck to the glass and the sheets from her school folders are on the desk. But she doesn't know what to do with Miss Laura's mobile; she doesn't know what to think. All she has to go on are the bits and pieces of information she overhears from the kitchen.

Her aunt had told her to go to her room, but this isn't her room. Even though this house is nicer than theirs in Ituzaingó and she likes having a window all to herself. A window she can climb through to go see the river and come back through without anyone knowing. One she can escape through if they find out what she did. She just has to jump over the iron gate in front of the house.

There's money in the bag.

She can climb through the window.

And go see the river.

Or go back to Buenos Aires.

It's a Tuesday, because yesterday they had the English quiz at school. She should be worried about her dad, but her main problem is what her mum will say if she finds Miss Laura's mobile. What everyone will say. What they'll do. Evelyn sees herself in a video in one of the school's WhatsApp groups.

Check out this video… If you found out your dad had died in a train crash, what would you do? Check this out too… If your daughter stole a mobile, what would you do? This is what happened to Evelyn, this is the exact moment she hears the news, this is the clip that's gone viral of Marta when she finds out her daughter stole Miss Laura's mobile, the exact moment when Marta first helps her escape and then beats the crap out of her.

They'll all laugh at the part where it says "beats the crap out of her" and will repeat it over and over. Just that part.

Because of a mobile. Because of a mobile she's going to miss Martín's birthday and her graduation trip. She doesn't know anyone here and only likes coming in the summer when they can go to the beach and swim in the river. Her aunt says that in the winter they can go to the thermal pools. Her mum says they're filthy. The river is gentle but you have to be careful. There are whirlpools that can drag you under, even if you know how to swim. The calmer it all seems, the more dangerous it is. Her mum and aunt are chatting quietly in the kitchen.

If her dad's alive, he'll have to be included in the plan. The three of them could go to Brazil. Or Paraguay. In Brazil, all the women in the jails are black and they braid each other's hair with different-coloured ribbons just like in YouTube videos. A blonde girl like Evelyn might be discriminated against, or maybe they'd elect her as leader or she'd become bisexual. Or maybe her mum could pay a fine. The problem is how to ask her all these questions. And where to keep Miss Laura's mobile. She can't ask her mum anything because she gets really mad. Though if you don't ask her, in the end she'll come and tell you.

On the desk, her aunt has different-coloured pens that say "Welcome to fabulous Las Vegas" in English, the letters in gold. Evelyn writes down a list of questions:

1. What did Dad do?
2. Are the police going to take him away?
3. Was there an accident?
4. What happened on the train?
5. Why did we leave?
6. Is Dad coming?
7. What if he's dead?
8. Are we in danger?
9. Are you mad?
10. At me or at Dad?

Her mum isn't going to want to answer this many questions. Which is why Evelyn crosses out numbers five to nine.

O LGA TRIPS on a loose paving stone and in an attempt not to fall, she steps on dog poop, slips half a metre and just manages to grab hold of a tree. She left the house in a frenzy and didn't bring the mobile phones. If she falls and breaks a bone, she won't be able to let Marta or anyone else know. Everything is a mess. And difficult. The pavement is all cracked. You can't even walk on it. And there's dog shit everywhere. Why doesn't anyone clean up their dog's turds? The day they get fined is when they'll do it. That or they won't have dogs. People are shits. Everything is about money.

Olga's day began poorly. She woke up sitting on the couch in front of the television. She'd spent the night like this, having fallen asleep watching the train situation. And now she realizes that Marta and Evelyn didn't call. Like they do every night, after the soap. Marta could have called, especially on a Monday night, when the whole neighbourhood knows Olga does the payment rounds. Marta does this sort of thing on purpose. She's headstrong. And so Olga goes over to check on them, because Marta isn't answering her messages and she's worried. Because Evelyn didn't stop by her house on the way to school.

Olga walks as quickly as she can. On top of everything, the rosewoods have blossomed early this year, and she slips on the yellow flowers beneath the smooth soles of her moccasins. Instead of planting trees they could station police officers. That way Olga would feel more comfortable with Evelyn going out on her own. Marta says it's just a few blocks. Her head is in the clouds. She won't even ask that lousy man she chose to be Evelyn's father to pick their daughter up from school. Olga's mind is racing, the 800 metres that separate her from Marta's house are a test of her athletic ability. And she left without breakfast. If Evelyn had a mobile, Olga could talk to her directly. But her mother doesn't want her to have one. Marta won't even listen to Olga about this. More than forty years and she still doesn't listen.

When Olga is a block away, she stops short on the pavement. She hesitates. Everything seems fine. If there was a fire, she'd have seen it from afar. It's got to be something else. She's afraid to keep going and discover the worst. To see them lying on the floor in a pool of blood. Or find the house empty without a trace of them. Today they kidnap women just like that. And they're never heard of again. But they wouldn't kidnap Marta. Why would they want Marta?

Olga squints her eyes to focus on the front of the house from a distance. There are no ambulances or fire engines. But there is a man at the door. She thinks about going back home and calling 911 but then she realizes he's a police officer. Something happened to them, she thinks.

She also thinks: "They've found us out."

H UGO LEAVES through the large door barefoot and in a stained shirt. No one sees him. It's already daylight out but the hospital casts a shadow over the parking lot at the entrance. He walks as upright as he can between people who rush towards anyone in a white lab coat. The police aren't there and neither is Marta. He reaches the car park, slips between the television production trucks and starts to jog. The wet grass puts out the fire raging in his feet. He crosses under the highway, protected by the dark, and picks up his pace until he reaches the maximum speed possible for a man who's just been in a crash. A few blocks later, having barely emerged from the panic and euphoria, he stops to breathe.

He looks around for a street name to situate himself. Pastor Obligado Street, right in the middle of the triangle the Posadas Hospital forms with Haedo and Ramos Mejía Stations. A dangerous area. He looks at himself in a car window. He's in pretty good shape. No blood on his face. Beto's house is a thousand blocks away, but his only option is to walk. Where else can he go?

There's 800 pesos in the jeans pocket. What a champ Alejo is. Now Hugo has bus fare. It's not theft, it's an accident. Just

74

like the train. Like Beto and Pamela and the motorcycle. Like Carlos David. None of it was on purpose.

Hugo looks for a bakery. He wants some croissants and decides there's not much of a risk: it's still too early for the police to be looking everywhere for him. If he hurries up, he can even play the lottery, put 300 pesos in Brinco. What number would he get for everything that happened today? 17,000.

He walks along minor streets, far from the main arteries. He tries to seem normal so no one looks at his feet. The paving stones feel harsh beneath them. So do the questions. About Marta, about Beto and about himself. Marta's smart. As for Beto, who knows at this point. He's also up to his neck in it. Beto was the one who wanted to get it all over with quick. Hugo would have preferred to have time to think, to do things better. And then maybe they wouldn't be in this mess now, maybe Hugo would have been able to go home and take care of his feet. Beto turned out to be so morbid. Because it's one thing to have an accident and another to be the person who thinks things through, who brings the bag and plans it all. Which of them is worse, in the end? If you think about it a little, Beto is frightening. What's worse? Now he needs to get some pastries and the two of them need to sit down together and think good and hard. For once.

It's been a while since Hugo crossed Rivadavia Avenue and he's feeling very queasy. He sits down on the kerb and puts his head between his knees. He smells like piss. And he's cold. And absolutely exhausted. He wants to know if

Evelyn is asking about him. He feels the urge to give up on this street corner and wait. For Marta, for Beto, for the police; whoever wants to find him first. He fantasizes that they're crying over him and he shows up with pastries like in a zombie movie. But the truth is Beto has to help because he's in this as well. Because it's all a big mistake. Because they're looking for him too. And because Hugo needs to know if Beto has talked.

C URIOSITY IS STRONGER than fear, which is why Olga decides to interrogate the police officer lurking outside Marta's house before he asks her any questions.

"Excuse me."

"Good morning, ma'am."

"Who are you?"

"What about you?"

"No one. But you're the police. What are you doing here?"

"You must be Mrs Marta Lacase's mother."

"No, I'm not. Why? What happened to her?"

"Come on, ma'am, you're like two peas in a pod."

"Did something happen?"

"I'm investigating a homicide. Don't be frightened," Domínguez says, though he can already see this woman is not easily frightened.

"What homicide? What are you saying? Marta didn't kill anybody."

"Actually, I'm looking for the man of the house."

"I'm a widow."

"I'm looking for Marta's husband. What's your name?"

"Olga Sanabria. Marta doesn't have a husband, there must be some mistake."

"Sure she does, Mr Hugo Víctor Lamadrid…"

"Oh, well, they're not married."

"Have you seen him? Or spoken to him?"

"What did he do?"

"Hasn't your daughter told you? Has she not called you?"

"Don't ask so many questions, you're making me very nervous. What's going on with Marta?"

"Nothing's going on—with Marta. Your son-in-law is suspected in a crime."

"Okay, but he's not my son-in-law."

"He may be among the victims of the train crash. Why don't we go inside? Do you have a key?"

"And do you have a warrant from a judge?"

"No, Olga, that's why I was ringing the bell and not knocking the door down."

"Did Hugo die in the train?"

"Ma'am, I don't want to make you nervous."

"Why do you want to go inside if you already know exactly what happened?"

Olga finally gives in and they enter the house. She hides her surprise well. "Can't you see there's nobody here?"

"Everything's a bit of a mess, Olga."

"Could someone have broken in? What if someone's taken my daughter and granddaughter?"

"Who?"

"I don't know, you tell me, you're the detective. What's your name?"

78

"Domínguez. Osvaldo Domínguez."

"I was expecting a name more… more… detective-like."

"Have a look in the closet. Is it possible there are things missing? Could they have gone somewhere?"

"Why are you asking me all this? I don't know, Marta's house is always a mess. What if they were kidnapped?"

"Has no one called you?"

"No! That's why I'm worried."

"Look, don't worry about that. This isn't a kidnapping."

Olga offers to make coffee and fortunately for her, Domínguez accepts. This gives her time to think. While the water drips through the filter, she picks up where she left off.

"So tell me, if Hugo's among the dead, what are you looking for here? Why don't you close the case and that's that?"

"He's not on the list of the dead, Olga. Though there are two unidentified bodies. We'll have to see if one of those is Hugo Víctor Lamadrid. There's not much to identify, truth be told. They're remains."

Olga moves her hand as though she were shooing flies away from a cadaver.

"And what about Marta? And the girl?"

"Why don't we call them and ask?"

"I didn't bring my mobile. I'm out of credit."

"Well, I can call her. Okay? And then I'll hand you the phone."

"Who's going to tell her about Hugo?"

"I already told her. About the homicide. Not about the bodies that haven't been identified. Not yet."

"And what did she say?"

"Nothing."

"You see?"

Bᴇᴛᴏ ᴊᴜᴍᴘꜱ at the sound of the doorbell. Every time it rings, he thinks of what's coming: the handcuffs, the jacket over his head, the whole neighbourhood cursing him, the TV lights following him until he's pushed into a police car. Hugo says that Beto watches too many series, that in real life news programmes aren't interested in Carlos David Cristaldo and neither is anyone else. He has no choice but to go see who's there—you can only pretend to be deaf for so long. On the other side of the door, Hugo shows him a box of pastries at a wide angle through the peephole. He should be feeling relief.

"Couldn't you have called before coming?"

"Thing is I lost my phone. But if you're with a broad, I'll leave."

Hugo finishes the feint with a half-turn but Beto pushes him inside the house, steps onto the pavement to see if anyone is watching them and slams the door shut. He already knows what's coming: Hugo's routine, wherein he minimizes everything, treats Beto like he's paranoid, pretends to be absent-minded. But not today.

"The police came to look for me. Don't tell me you didn't know." Hugo points to Beto with his other hand, the one not holding the pastries.

Beto is silent as he looks Hugo in the eye. It's all getting more complicated. This is what happens when you're not a professional, when you're an idiot who acts without thinking. Hugo's eyes are sunken into a face with greenish, taut skin, its bones straining to come out. He's still pointing his accusatory finger and holding up the box of pastries. Beto points at him too, with a play gun he forms between his index finger and thumb.

"You forgot I'm on a diet."

"You've turned into a fag."

They stand there face to face, sizing each other up, like in a western, until Beto starts to notice the details. Hugo is barefoot. His shirt is destroyed, his trousers are stained and his gaze is drifting. Yet again, Hugo has lost control. Yet again, Beto is going to have to think for the two of them, take charge, find the tools, come up with some excuse to get the bag from Marta, speed down the highway, the bag tied to the motorcycle as best he can, run with the dead weight, looking for that piece of shit creek, while Hugo goes back home so they don't have any problems. And on top of everything, here he is suggesting that Beto's fucking with him. It's all so unacceptable he doesn't know where to begin.

"You're afraid I'm gonna talk to the cops and you go to La Estrella de Galicia to buy pastries? You're in a bakery at eight in the morning with your trousers covered in blood?"

"I didn't know," Hugo says, his eyes searching as though

for the bottom of a pit. He finally lowers the box of pastries and looks for a chair. "Do you know what post-traumatic stress is? I think I have that."

"You're a fool."

Beto offers Hugo some coffee and he asks for milk with it. They open the box of pastries and Hugo quickly snatches up the one he'd chosen beforehand, and while he chews, he puts his story in order: the train, the conversation with St Expeditus, the message from Marta, the rescue.

"It was on Crónica TV. They pulled everyone out through the roof. But I didn't see you."

"Well, sorry I didn't say hello."

Beto's anger is transforming into what it always does with Hugo, who's now crying because no one called him all night to see if he was okay.

"You lost your phone, how do you know no one called you?"

"You're right. You're the one who thinks clearly."

In the past, when Hugo said this he was praising Beto. Now it seems a lot like an accusation. Beto doesn't understand if his friend has showed up to hide out, to drag him down with him, or both. Though it's most likely he doesn't have a plan. For a change.

"You need to see a doctor, something could be broken. Remember Pamela?"

"I don't ever forget. What happened with Pamela really changed you... Now you're cold-blooded. Because I fucked up, but you... you were chill."

83

Beto processes the information and the meta message. He's done talking. He has to go to work and tells Hugo he can stay for a few days. Like he has a choice. Beto leaves him a set of keys, tells him not to open the door for anybody, and to stop talking bullshit.

I N THE STUDIO, Sandra Lagos is talking to the camera but making eye contact with the family members behind it, waiting among the cables. It's not clear how she manages this. Marina offers the elderly woman and the young man some coffee while they look for the photos she requested and send them to her on WhatsApp. They didn't go through make-up. That would have been disrespectful. El Rifle has stopped bugging her. No doubt he's gone for a run.

The truth is that the topic had been exhausted before the day began. The list had been made known in the early hours. Marina checks the phone numbers she's gotten, thinks that maybe there'll be a wake in the afternoon. Nothing's going on at the hospital entrance. The doctors won't be coming out until midday—the programme will have to wait until then to learn if anyone can be saved or might die. Those with minor injuries spoke to the first production truck.

The family members are now talking among themselves, telling each other how they found out. Marina apologizes and asks them if they can speak quietly, she apologizes again and promises that it'll just be a little longer before they can leave, then she apologizes again. People have gathered at the station but they have nothing to say. The programme will have to wait for the candles and flowers. They'll have to wait for everything.

Sandra Lagos approaches the elderly woman and the young man. She greets them by touching the woman's shoulder and shaking the man's hand. The cameras turn to the living room where the three of them take a seat. When the lights are turned on and they begin to speak, Marina leaves the studio and goes to the control room. She looks at the other channels on the monitors. They're showing onlookers at the station and the wreck of a carriage under the morning sun. No one is on the platform. No one is at the hospital entrance. The hosts of other programmes look like they're talking to civil servants on the phone. Sandra Lagos asks the family members whether anyone from the government has called them. Everything is under way now. Marina gets herself a cup of coffee and eats the croissant she's been avoiding. On WhatsApp, El Rifle asks her for the phone number of the two people who are on air.

E VELYN LEAVES the "study" and walks through the hallway to the kitchen. Marta wants to change the topic but can't think of another one. Mónica changes it for her.

"I went to Las Vegas."

Her sister and niece stare at her in disbelief.

"Las Vegas, North America."

"I know where Las Vegas is. But when was this? You didn't tell me anything."

"Marta, we haven't talked in months. Until last night when you sent me a WhatsApp message saying you were coming."

"Well, you don't have to throw it in my face. We'll leave as soon as we can."

"That's not it! You're the one who threw my not telling you in my face."

"Well then, tell me."

"They sent me as compensation for presenteeism."

"Explain what that is to Evelyn… Your aunt never misses work and they rewarded her with a trip to Las Vegas."

"I got it, Mum… So where did the plane leave from? Did they hire a car to take you to Buenos Aires?"

"Yes. I took a van straight from here to the plane in Buenos Aires, like a queen."

"Seriously, they sent you in a car from here? What, are you doing it with some bingo boss?"

"It was a van. And it's nothing like that. I told you it was compensation for presenteeism. Also, it's not a bingo hall. It's a casino."

"Aunt Mónica, was it summer when you went? Was there a swimming pool?"

"I don't know, everything is air-conditioned there. I don't know what season it was… I went in August."

"Look at your aunt, Evelyn! Las Vegas! You didn't go and get married, did you? How long were you there? Just a week?"

"Three hours." The look of disappointment on her sister's face irritates Mónica. "I didn't have a visa, what do you expect? I got my passport, but not the visa. And they wanted me to leave in two days to go to this presentation for a machine."

"So then you went to work! What kind of compensation is that, Mónica?"

"It's compensation. Do you think they send just anyone to Las Vegas? The thing is you haven't been on the job market for a long time, you don't know how competitive it is."

Mónica knows her jab was more painful than Marta's but now there's no going back. Either she keeps talking or Evelyn asks what happened to her dad.

"They chose me because I have a good understanding of how the machines work. You have no idea what this one was like. It's the latest generation."

"But couldn't you have stayed a few days?" Marta asks grudgingly.

"The casino obtained special permission from the embassy—at the highest level. But without a visa you can't remain on US territory for more than twelve hours."

"Aunt Mónica, did you watch a movie on the plane?"

"I sure did."

"Which one?"

"The one you liked… the one with that pale boy, the skinny one… You told me about it on your communion day."

"That was a long time ago."

"Evelyn, let your aunt talk about Las Vegas."

"Oh, it's beautiful. Everything's impeccable, including the airport. It's all very well-organized. I arrived and they put me in this impressive van. And then we drove to Las Vegas. You have no idea what it's like… it's like going to Europe and the United States at the same time. I went to Paradise… Paradise… it's name was Paradise something. They brought me in through the back door, because it was a surprise—me being at the presentation. But you have no idea what the back door was like. A thousand times better than the front door of any hotel here. A luxury. I was in a rush because the presentation had already begun. I made myself up as best I could, I had horrific bags under my eyes after the flight, I was dying to pee. The machine was covered with a cloth and when they gave me the signal, I went in surrounded by all those lights and I uncovered it, like it was a monument. Then they began to show me all the functions.

The man went on about each of them in English and even though I don't speak a word, I followed him perfectly. It was like it had been rehearsed. It was magic."

"So did you see anyone famous?" Evelyn asks, clearly bored.

"A bunch of people."

"Who!?"

"I don't know their names, but they were famous for sure."

The sound of Marta's phone brings them back from Las Vegas. The three of them sit there in silence, looking at the device. It's an unknown number.

"It's ringing, Mum."

"Let it ring, it's not important."

"What if it's Dad?"

B ETO HASN'T OPENED the shop. He's in the café on the corner, glancing sidelong at the television. It's his third cup of coffee and the morning has just begun. The excess of caffeine has taken effect in his restless leg and speeding mind. The television is on mute. The only sound is Beto's teaspoon clinking against his plate every time his nervous knee hits the table.

Crónica TV is replaying images from the train rescue. They were taken with a zoom of more than a hundred metres in the middle of the night. You can't see anything—just blue shadows. It could be as fake as man landing on the moon. Beto is among those who are convinced the moon landing was all a set-up. It's his favourite topic of debate with Hugo. Hugo believes the whole spectacle. "You would have made a great journalist," Beto tells Hugo to hurt him. They both know that's not true. At some point all of their conversations became this bitter and cruel.

The problem with Hugo is that he had high expectations and now his fuck-ups are as massive as his frustration. Beto, on the other hand, was always just interested in getting by. So he decides to limit himself to this.

W HEN THE PHONE began to ring, they kicked Evelyn out of the kitchen again. Which is fine for her, she has things to do. Now that her mum and aunt are busy again, it's a good time to hide Miss Laura's mobile well. But where? Where can she put it? Everything is so tidy at her aunt's place that hiding it behind or inside something would be impossible. Everything looks nice and is organized, it's a mystery she never married with a house like this.

The wardrobe in the "study" has two shelves full of the products her aunt sells. Some of the boxes are the size of a mobile. Evelyn sees them as the only option. And the lesser evil: if her aunt ends up selling one of the gadgets and there's a mobile inside the box, there's no way the woman who buys it will complain. She finds an X-acto knife in the desk and carefully opens one of the biggest boxes. She already knows what's inside it, but she's still surprised when she takes it out. It's got to be a mistake. Or decorative. It doesn't say *consolador* anywhere on the box. It says "vibrator". In English. "What the fuck!" Evelyn says, the words coming out in English too. The vibrator is very large.

Her mum and aunt are still busy, so before she hides the evidence, Evelyn examines the thing a little. She looks for a ruler and measures it. Seventeen and a half. Martín says that when he gets hard it's like twenty, so she figures they must come in even bigger sizes. The box doesn't say anything about the size. She guesses it's a "medium". Martín is always saying that one day she'll have to do it for the first time and it's going to hurt. Evelyn is surprised they sell them like this—hard. She likes the colour. She can't avoid the memory of the guy who showed her his when she was leaving school. It was really gross, way grosser than this. Or that's what the other girls said, because Evelyn covered her eyes. She was the only one who didn't look, and now they all know what a dick is like except for her.

She puts Miss Laura's mobile in the box but she doesn't know what to do with the vibrator. It's no use: both won't fit. She really doesn't know where to put it. It's too big for everything, even her pencil case. And a mouth—how do women put them in their mouths if they're bigger than hot dogs? That's why Martín's sister gagged the first time she sucked one. There are noises coming from the kitchen. Evelyn is afraid they'll see her. She hides the vibrator in the pocket of her sweatshirt and runs to the bathroom.

Mónica is offended by the Las Vegas conversation. She's in the kitchen, putting things away with her back to Marta. Evelyn isn't making any noise. The sound of the phone reverberates in the silent room. Night has been over for a while and something has to happen. Marta insists on remaining calm. When she answers the call, whatever it is that's happening is going to overwhelm her with the fury of the sunlight entering through the window and filling the whole space. Mónica tires of this, grabs the device, presses the green button, hands the phone to her sister and returns to what she was doing.

Olga regrets not having her phones with her. The police officer is in control of the situation and all she'll be able to do is add a few comments. When Marta picks up, Domínguez signals to Olga with his hand, telling her to be patient. But he's too late.

"Quick, say something before she hangs up," Olga orders him.

"Mum?" Marta recognizes the voice on the other end of the phone.

"No. It's Detective Domínguez."

"Ask her where she is," Olga calls out, wanting to direct the interrogation.

"If you're looking for Hugo, he left early," Marta says, making things up as she goes.

Domínguez gets to his feet and begins to pace, staring at the floor, distancing the phone from Olga, searching among the tiles for the right words to tell Marta she's making a mess of things and at the same time to ensure she doesn't get away from him. He asks for her cooperation. Says there's no need to lie, since she's not a suspect. He just has a few short questions and she'll be able to talk to her mother.

"Don't put my mother on. I'm at my sister's in Colón."

Mónica is incensed. She gesticulates with her head, her hand, her whole body to say no, and out of pure helplessness, she slams the kettle on the stove and empties the *mate*, making noise to emphasize her disapproval.

"To Mónica's! Has she gone mad!? Evelyn has to go to school! Marta, listen, this man is investigating a crime Hugo committed. It seems…" Olga yells over Domínguez's left shoulder. The detective has turned away from her and moved into a corner to try to get the situation under control.

He's surrounded. He decides to deal with what's essential for now and asks Marta if she knows anything about her husband, whether he's called or she's had news. Olga protests, says her daughter is not married, and that since Hugo never calls, he's not exactly going to call after he's committed a crime. She tells him to be reasonable. As best he can, Domínguez informs Marta of what she already knows: Hugo is not dead or wounded and he has not been detained, at least not on paper. He also tells her what she doesn't know: that there are unidentified remains no one has claimed.

Marta clings to her last resort in an attempt at simplifying things.

"But if he was on the train, don't you think that…"

"Give me the phone!" Olga orders him.

"Ma'am, give her a call later," says Domínguez, trying to evade Olga's swipes, returning to Marta. "It's likely they'll have to conduct a DNA test. On your daughter Evelyn, as you're aware."

Mónica offers her sister a sip of the *mate* she's just prepared and gives her a look as though to say be careful what you do. The hit of adrenaline mixed with hot water, *mate* and sugar takes effect. It brings all of the factors involved into focus. Marta thinks quickly and clearly. And she surprises herself:

"This is your problem. Hugo got away from you, not me."

"Marta's right about that," Olga chimes in. "He's dead to us. Tell me it's not better for everyone that way."

O NE OPTION is to face the situation. Surrender to the police and talk before Beto does. Tell them what happened. An argument with Carlos David that got out of hand. The kid, poor guy, he started it, he was a little violent. It wasn't on purpose. Not entirely not on purpose, but let's say the outcome was unplanned. And then, a series of erroneous decisions to protect a friend. Because Beto, Alberto Luis Morales, has no record, nothing. It's an option—telling them what happened. With a little licence, small changes to the script. But essentially giving them what they need. It's not like they're going to care about the details.

Hugo is in the shower, the water washing away the traces of oil, filth and dried blood, while he considers his options and his body. He turns his head from side to side, forms a four with his legs, balancing on one and bending the other, then closes an eye and tries to touch the end of his nose with his left index finger, before doing the same with the right. It's what he usually does to show Marta he's not drunk. Now it's a way of checking there's no neurological damage. He got off easy. But not free. They'll give him a few months in the slammer.

He stays under the hot water a little longer. Beto has a good shower. He lives pretty well. Makes enough to get by, has all his time to himself. Beto's life has always been the same; it's just that now, in comparison, it seems better than Hugo's.

Hugo leaves the bathroom without drying off and looks for a bin bag. In it, he puts his filthy shirt, jeans covered in blood—which could be his or that kid Alejo's—and pissed-in briefs. Everything reeks. He can't remember if he pissed himself in the carriage or at the hospital. He ties the bag and leaves it next to the front door. Still starkers, he stops in his tracks in the middle of the dining room, so he doesn't frighten away an idea that flies by stealthily, not wanting to be caught. Beto has taken the pastries with him. He was in a rush to get to work. Beto's become so selfish. The idea gets away from Hugo without taking shape. That's why he never learnt to write well. He's pure intuition and argumentative noise.

The only thing he knows is that they're looking for him. And not for Beto. And that between killing Carlos David and everything that happened after, there's not much difference. Killing someone, cutting up a body to put it into a bag, throwing that body into a creek—it's all the same. They're both going to be arrested. If one of them wants to go to the police to negotiate, he's going to need something better than a story about a couple of wretches who fuck-up one thing after another.

S EATED IN FRONT of the detective, Olga tears off a piece of paper towel and folds it in two, four, eight, while he downs his second coffee, which is already lukewarm. She stops him when he gets up to leave.

"Why do you want to make this complicated and get the girl involved?"

Olga speaks fluently, without stopping; she's not about to let Domínguez take advantage of a pause to get away. She tries to talk some sense into him. "Two plus two is four," she repeats, while she presses her nail into one of the folds in the paper towel. Whose bodies would they be if not Hugo's? There's only one person that nobody can find. He's not here, not in the hospital, not anywhere. It's him if nobody's claimed those bodies. It's him. It has to be. It's too great a coincidence. If other families hadn't found the bodies of their relatives, they'd be on television by now, creating a scandal. If she wasn't here, cooperating with the investigation, but had gone to file a report, what would the head of police have told her? That it's him. The police wouldn't go spending money on analyses: they would have given her a body, told her it was Hugo, and that would have been that. With all the people waiting for assistance, and all the work

99

the police have with so many robberies, kidnappings, crimes, a case solves itself and Domínguez wants to complicate it.

The detective starts explaining procedures to Olga. He realizes he's fallen into her trap as he's eating a piece of supermarket cake and drinking his third coffee. Olga doesn't understand why they're dedicating so many resources to a minor case.

"The kid Hugo killed, you said he was Paraguayan, right? Isn't this a problem for the police in Paraguay then?"

Olga is thinking about what's best for everyone. Because if Evelyn's father did what they say he did, why are they trying to find him? It's not that she's defending Hugo—that's not it at all. Domínguez doesn't know her; if he did, he'd know she never liked Hugo. Marta doesn't make good choices, Domínguez, Olga thinks, look at what she did: she picked up and left. Someone needs to resolve this, because Hugo is her granddaughter's father. This is an excellent opportunity for Evelyn—that is, if the detective can understand.

"Do you have grandchildren, Domínguez?"

"No, I married but we didn't have children. Though I'm divorced now."

"Are you a workaholic?"

"A bit of one."

Domínguez stays a little longer. Because the way Olga is playing with her words, suggesting he leave things as they are, amuses and intrigues him. The woman is right: it's for the best. For Hugo and for the remains that don't belong to anyone, for Marta and her mother, for Evelyn and for the department head. For him, because he let a suspect escape from a place nobody got away from on their own, and because he would be a suspect himself if anyone were to find out about the mobile.

And yet, the convenience of it makes him uncomfortable. It's true he's a workaholic. It's not about the truth or integrity or justice, about what's right, and other ambitions of that sort. It's something that's stronger than him. The necessity to close the circle, to have everything fit. That's what it is. Nothing else. And in this case, the pieces have become increasingly scattered, like the pieces of the bodies no one has been able to put back together.

"And are you certain there are two bodies? How do they know?" Olga asks, before telling Domínguez it would be better if he didn't say anything else, so as not to upset her.

MARTA AND MÓNICA are able to agree when necessary. They have two options: believe that Hugo is alive and remain in the kitchen, unable to act, brooding over everything bad that could happen, until he shows up, or trust that he's dead and try to get their lives in order—the house, Evelyn's school, money and everything else that needs to be done. They choose the second option without much debate, their voices hushed, half their attention on the movements beyond the hallway, to make sure Evelyn is busy and can't hear them. That's how Marta realizes her daughter is in the bathroom crying. She can still sense when Evelyn is crying—it's the sort of ability that makes her feel she's a good mum despite everything.

Evelyn also senses that something's up. She presses a button and all the blood is flushed away. She dries her tears and hurries to open the door. Though she can walk, it hurts. It feels like she's been pinched a thousand times at once. Marta hugs her. She promises they'll go back to Buenos Aires to say goodbye to her father and that everything will be all right. It's only then that she asks her daughter what happened. Evelyn clings to the decidedly convenient misunderstanding and reinforces it by saying that on top of everything she got her period and her stomach hurts. But Mónica recognizes what's poking out of the cloth bag bordered in lace, which is where she keeps her cotton balls.

"Evelyn, that's a Long Pleasure 9000! Where did you get that?"

Mónica reaches for the Long Pleasure and holds it with the tip pointing upwards, as though she were reproaching a little thief for what she'd just stolen. Marta tries to decide who to be angry at. Evelyn doesn't say anything.

"You don't want to begin with this, Evelyn!"

That's when Marta explodes.

"She shouldn't be beginning with anything, Mónica! What are you saying?"

Evelyn understands that if she holds back the tears, the pain and the fear, it'll stay between her mum and aunt. She keeps her mouth shut and tries to get away from the limited space under the door frame between the bathroom and the hallway, where the three of them are standing. There's a painful silence. A train crash is nothing compared to this. Evelyn's aunt is now pointing the Long Pleasure at her, right between her eyes.

"Evelyn, this isn't for you. You're very young. This is very big. Did you use it?"

Marta doesn't wait for an answer. She tells her daughter to go finish her English homework. Evelyn protests—why study if they left and she doesn't have school any more? Mónica tells her to please not open any more boxes.

"This one's no good now, I won't be able to sell it. But if you keep it…"

"Shut up, Mónica, she's a child."

Evelyn goes into her room.

"It's not worth making such a fuss over," says Mónica.

She turns around, opens the bathroom faucet, pushes the soap dispenser and washes the gadget as though she were giving a hand job. Marta lingers on this detail, but now is not the time to ask her sister if she's finally jerked some guy off.

"It's not a man, it's a vibrator. You let her have Facebook, where some stranger could deceive her, where anything could happen, but she comes across this in my house, a family member's house, and this is how you react? Do you know what she's doing on Facebook? Don't you realize it's dangerous?"

"What if she hurts herself with your *consolador*, Mónica?"

"It's a vibrator, vi-bra-tor, people don't say *consolador* any more."

"You think I care what people say? She could hurt herself, it's dangerous."

"It's men that are dangerous, Marta."

T HE TROUSERS and crumpled black T-shirt that Hugo finds on the chair next to the bed are too big on all sides. Beto has gotten fat—his head and his body. Hugo also borrows a backpack. There's room in it for other things he gets from the closet: a pair of trousers—he can't decide whether they're long shorts or short jeans—a couple of T-shirts with the brand names of motorcycle accessories on them, a sweatshirt with the Ferrari logo on it. He rummages through Beto's drawers and night table, but doesn't find any money. Then he checks the jars in the cupboard and that's where he finds the bills. Beto acts just likes an old man. Hugo divides the loot between the front pocket of Beto's trousers and the bottom of the backpack. Before he leaves the room, he gets Beto's ID card and transit pass.

Coffee, a shower and movement do one good. Before Hugo leaves, he wants to watch the news, but there are two or three remote controls on the table and he doesn't know which one to use. The screen is almost as big as the wall and doesn't have any buttons that might resolve the matter. Apparently they don't make televisions with on and off buttons any more. Beto has been gone for more than an hour. If he'd wanted to turn Hugo in to the police, they'd already be there. For a moment, Hugo considers trusting Beto and negotiating together. Asking to speak to whoever's in charge, offering to be protected witnesses for something drug related and turning in the old bitch. First they'd have to find out how it works: if you sign that everything is kept confidential and no one knows who you are. Witness A, Witness B, Witness X. Hugo's seen the statement appear this way in the papers. It might even pay a couple of pesos.

But the modern television is a nuisance and he's furious with Beto for having it. He manages to turn the device on but the volume startles him and drives him mad until he finally manages to control that button as well. Beto has no desire to grow. As soon as he earns a bit of money, he buys himself a millionaire's television and a motorcycle. He doesn't look to the future. It remains to be determined whether he'd be up to challenging Olga. He'd rather work for her than make decisions—Beto is not one for taking initiative. He's afraid of her. It's easier for him to be a soldier, pick up a bit of cash on Mondays and spend it on a television fit for NASA, so that Hugo can't figure out how to change the channels when he wants to watch the recap of the Tigre match. That sonofabitch Beto, who can't just have a normal television, who went and raised his standard of living just like that and thinks no one's going to find out. Beto is dangerous, maybe more so than Olga, who after all is family.

El Rifle Barrios is on TV and Hugo stops trying to change channels—he figures El Rifle's programme might show the Tigre match. But it doesn't: when the football segment comes on, only the best matches are recapped, which are the ones they give El Rifle. On the politics programme, it's all National B, Tigre's league. There are three blokes no one knows on El Rifle's programme. They'd been asked on for something else but ended up talking about the accident. It's a repeat from last night. It wasn't long ago that Hugo saw El Rifle. They were at a barbecue with the other guys in their group, the ones who still get together after twenty years. When he got home, he fought with Marta. He had to take it out on someone. El Rifle had that look on his face of having just gotten laid, like he does every other day. He had on his pointy shoes, was tanned in the middle of winter after covering the World Cup and spent the meal complaining that everything had gone to shit, that everything was a disaster. How lucky Huguito was, he said, to do something else for a living, to have saved himself from the madness; how lucky he was to have the quality of life he did, to move at a different speed, one that was more humane, to go home and have a family waiting. This was El Rifle's coked-out monologue, the condescension more humiliating than the rejection. There's no way Hugo is going to turn himself in and give El Rifle the satisfaction of saying he knows him well.

He leaves the TV on and puts the bag of clothes from the

accident in the backpack so he can toss it out somewhere. A St Expeditus holy card hangs from the peephole inside the front door. He borrows this too, putting it in the back pocket of the baggy trousers, and he leaves.

OLGA ALSO has a St Expeditus holy card hanging from the peephole in her front door. Through it, she observes Beto's face at a wide angle.

"What are you doing here?"

She opens the door to say this and is already closing it when he stops her with his hand.

"It's urgent. Hugo came over and..."

Olga shuts Beto's mouth with a look and pushes him inside while she checks both ways along the street. Fortunately, no one has seen them. She's furious because Beto and the others are not allowed to come to her house. But even more so because of his news.

"The idiot's not dead?"

"No."

"The two of you are a pain in the neck."

Beto stammers that he brought pastries and Olga grabs the box from his hands, while reproaching him for everything he already knows. She tells him he's an idiot for showing up at her house like that, an idiot for having involved Hugo in the business and mixing family with work; she says he's also an idiot for not stopping Hugo when he wanted to go it alone, and for helping him with Carlos David; and a major idiot for opening the door and leaving him there in his home. And what's more, she says, Hugo is an idiot who can't do anything right, not even die.

"Olga, with all due respect, your daughter Marta's also in the business."

"Don't be an idiot. Marta and I have another venture that has nothing to do with this and doesn't concern you. Don't involve yourself with my family. It's the last time I'll tell you. Do something about Hugo—you're the one who got him into this. He screwed everything up."

"But Hugo is part of your family too, isn't he?"

Olga chokes down another dozen "idiots" that build up in her throat. She doesn't let them out. Everything Beto says irritates her further. He's an idiot. But he's the only idiot she can count on now. Domínguez didn't say anything about him. It's likely that Beto doesn't exist for the police.

"I should have fired you a long time ago."

Beto gives up on Olga inviting him in to take a seat and on their discussing what to do next. He understands he won't be able to ask her if they're looking for him too. She leaves everything in a state of limbo, is all suggestions without specific instructions in what is the most terrifying of situations for Beto: having to make decisions. As Olga opens the door, she gives him one more piece of information:

"A detective from the homicide department is looking for Hugo. I'd never seen him before. He left me his card. Domínguez, a gentleman."

IT'S THE ONLY THING they're talking about on television. Olga is clicking through the channels. She's seated in the carob wood chair she bought when she sold everything from the wedding, and sipping on a mug of tea with milk. A kid who's just left emergency at the Posadas Hospital is talking about the train crash. He says he thought he was going to die, and Olga changes to another news channel. The same kid seen from a different angle is saying that he heard a loud noise. "A loud noise like in a normal crash or louder?" he's asked. Olga puts on Sandra Lagos's programme, which she watches every morning because she likes the host, and there's the same kid saying, "No, it wasn't like a normal crash." On this channel, you can see the side of his head that's bandaged. The kid lucked out. Olga is bored. It's all minor injuries and people giving their opinions on television. Everything quickly becomes old news.

She opens the box of pastries Beto brought. There are three in it, not one of which is a croissant. Beto is a wretch. And he's also dangerous. She can't decide between the rectangular pastry with a circle of custard in its centre and the puff pastry. The third option is a squashed bun covered in burnt brown sugar. "Given the circumstances, *el vigilante* is the best bet," Olga says out loud, chuckling quietly at her joke before taking a bite of the puff pastry known as "the watchman" and looking through the contacts on her phone.

It's also the only thing they're talking about in the neighbourhood. No one seems to have seen the police car at Marta's house the night before. Otherwise Fabio would have asked her about it when she put credit on her phone at the convenience store. Olga pushes the green button and on the other end a police officer she does know answers.

B ETO ARRIVES at the shop half an hour late and the client who ordered the Hawk is waiting for him. He starts talking about his motorcycle while Beto raises the blinds and tries to be pleasant, though his mind is elsewhere, on the early events of the morning. The helmet has been ready for the client since yesterday. He tries it on and looks at himself in the mirror, face on and in profile, his hands raised in front of him, as though he were gripping the bike's handlebars, his legs slightly flexed.

"It'll keep you very safe," Beto says mechanically.

"Looks good, doesn't it?" the biker asks into the air.

"Looks cool," Beto says, and his legs tremble a little because he's thinking that both him and Hugo are going to fuck things up.

"Did you see what happened to the train? And they say bikes are dangerous."

The fat man covered in leather is in the mood to chat, and with his helmet still on, he looks at jackets, backpacks, glasses and parts, and asks how much everything costs. Beto wants the man to leave so he can think. Before Hugo and Olga think on his behalf. He turns on the shop's television and right away he regrets it, because the pain in the neck with the helmet stays to watch the news.

"THIS IS THE VERY LATEST in lubricant gels. The newest flavours. Chocolate Passion, Menthol XXX, Little Red Riding Hood's Berries. They're incredible, they won't let you down. This is scientifically proven. Because they contain pheromones. Does anyone know what pheromones are? Nobody wants to answer. You're a shy group today. Feel free to give them a try. Just a drop or two. And be careful, because when you go out, the men will be on your tails in the street. A little goes a long way. And they're really not expensive. Have a look at the expiry date, one bottle will last a year. Though you want to try to use it up before then, am I right? So nobody knows what pheromones are. Ladies, come on, it's in all the magazines. It's like a… a… substance… but you can't see it… it's in our hormones… or, it's… how can I explain it to you… it's what attracts the opposite sex. Like a perfume that you smell without realizing it. I'm not saying men will be able to smell them, it's at a subconscious level. That goes for the pheromones, the rest of the gel he will be aware of because of the flavour. They taste very good, not too sweet. Put a bit on your hand and give it a try. Chocolate won't let you down. It's an aphrodisiac. I'm serious, there are scientific studies. The idea is to help yourselves out a little, invent new things. You might ask him to put the berries flavour... The gel, ladies, the gel goes first! You can't go skipping steps, this is for foreplay. If you buy two, there's a promo, you'll get a twenty per cent discount. Chocolate and berries, the perfect dessert! And I have these edible thongs that..."

"What about menthol?"

"Hold on a minute, Marta."

"But you started talking about the thongs and you didn't say anything about the menthol gel."

"Don't be so uptight, you have to let things flow. They give you a script but you also have to put a bit of your personality into selling."

Evelyn is trying to fall asleep with a pillow between her legs. Her aunt is talking like a TV host, like Evelyn's teacher does when she gives a speech outside, in a voice that comes from the kitchen and resounds throughout the house. Her mum's voice is just a whisper when it reaches her. She had looked Evelyn in the eye and said, "I'm not going to be mad, tell me what you did," but Evelyn could tell she was mad. Now she's listening to her aunt and understands that maybe with chocolate gel things would have turned out better. Her mum wanted to believe her when she said she didn't do anything wrong with her aunt's vibrator, and things calmed down right away. She's waiting for the pain to pass. Or to get used to it. This, at least, is a pain she can feel and comprehend. An easy pain.

"Have a look at the bottle—it looks like perfume. That's not a thing men will notice, but it matters to us women. If I bring you this very hypoallergenic gel, with imported essences, only it's in what looks like a mayonnaise container, it's not the same, am I right? We take these kinds of things in through our eyes, and that's very important when it comes to sex. As for the Menthol XXX, give it a try, it's like ice. Only less dangerous, since an ice cube straight from the freezer could stick to you. Rub it and it'll give you goose bumps. Because sometimes a woman's not entirely in the mood and this helps…"

"How does it help, Mónica, because I used it once and I froze? The ceiling fan was on and I nearly died."

"It must not have been this product. It's the best on the market, you have no idea how it sells."

"Do you really think this does anything for guys? Men don't like berries."

Mónica fans herself with the sex-toy flyer. It's the third disagreement they've had this morning. And Marta has just arrived. Plus the Hugo situation isn't going to be over any time soon.

"I'm offering you my clients so you can start something. Don't be so negative."

"It's that I feel like a complete idiot making the jokes. The gel grosses me out a little, and the chewable thongs…"

"Edible."

"Well, how do you eat them? You chew them, don't you?"

Evelyn hears her mum and aunt laugh and it's then that she's able to fall asleep. Marta looks through the catalogue of vibrators and wants to know if her sister has used all of them.

"I've tested all of the products. What are you laughing at me for? Are you so sure it was better with Hugo?" Mónica closes the kitchen door. It's better to say everything and to say it now. "Do you want to go back to Ituzaingó to take on Hugo's mess and have the police after you? Back to selling drugs with Mum?"

For the first time in a long while, Marta doesn't avert her gaze from her sister's eyes. Olga's genes are apparent in both of them at this moment.

"You're right about all but one thing: I'm not involved in Mum's business. I sold pills, but you can relax because I'm not going to keep doing it."

"What pills?"

"You'll get mad if I tell you. Show me the thongs."

"Something illegal, no doubt."

"No. Women take them now, when they have an accident. They put them in there."

"I don't understand."

"Yes, you do, when you sell the gels you say 'in there' all the time."

"By the holy wounds!"

"Enough with the rosary, Mónica. Do you know what it's like to get pregnant and not want to be?"

"I don't run that risk."

TWO TAXIS are waiting for the family members, as is Marina, who invites them back the next day. They say they'll let her know. The last of the wounded passengers to leave the emergency room at Posadas has spoken to all the cameras. There are now no more injured. At the station, it's only relatives of relatives and friends of friends. No direct family members. People have begun to protest yet another train accident, but none are the true protagonists. They're not the ones who tried to climb down from the platform, desperate to find a piece of someone, or the ones who hugged those who came out alive, or cried alone on the kerb outside the morgue. Those people wandered in front of the cameras all night long, until the sun came up, and each learnt what it was that chance had in store for them.

"But who saw them at that hour? You're not going to get anything done like this."

Sandra Lagos is talking as she walks along the hallway between the studio and make-up. Marina is following her, looking at her phone and suggesting options. Sandra could call three or four family members to come in tomorrow. Also someone from the government and the opposition. And there's the union.

"We're not going to argue over who's guilty on my programme. This is where people come to seek justice."

Marina says okay. They stop to watch the TV in the make-up room. At Haedo Station, there are already bouquets of flowers, photographs of some of the dead and a heavy silence.

OLGA HAS STOPPED paying attention to the TV. There's nothing new on, it's all boring. She looks for Domínguez's card and calls the number.

"Why didn't you tell me you found Hugo's things on the train?"

"This is the first I've heard of it, Olga. I'm not involved in the operation. Who called you? What did they find?"

"I have information off the record that they found a wallet with his ID in it."

"That's exactly why Marta needs to come in and…"

"It's clear as can be, Domínguez!"

"No, ma'am, until they identify those bodies, we can't be sure."

"I don't know why you want to deal with so much paperwork. I'm going to do what needs to be done."

Olga ends the conversation and Domínguez wonders what it is that needs to be done. He thinks it would be best to head to her neighbourhood and ask around about her.

She turns the television's volume on maximum and half-listening to the news, takes a clothes hanger with a garment cover from the closet. On it is a Chanel-style blazer and a matching pair of black trousers. She hasn't worn these items in years, but they fit well. She's still the same size. Her purse is in a cloth bag, her dark glasses in their case in the night table.

Standing in front of the mirror, she thinks for a moment: it hasn't been that long since she wore the suit. The last time was at Evelyn's communion. "With those glasses," Hugo told her, "you look like Isabelita Perón did when she was in Madrid."

"Isn't she still in Madrid?" Olga responded.

Marta thought Isabelita had died and Evelyn asked who she was. But Evelyn also told Olga she looked pretty. And Mónica started to talk about Peronism and got into an argument with Hugo. Her daughters have no sense of humour. Or character. Olga has to make decisions for everyone, like always.

She wraps the square pastry with custard and the bun with brown sugar in the paper they came in. She's about to toss the whole box away, but instead puts it in her purse along with her mobile, Domínguez's card, the picture frame with Evelyn's communion photo and the keys to Marta's house. At the taxi stand, they give her a bit of trouble when she asks to go to Haedo Station. Doesn't she know what happened? they ask. It'll be hell trying to get there with so many people milling about—impossible. But since Olga is a frequent traveller, the man in charge tells her, they'll make an exception. In the end, they get there quickly. No one wants to go in that direction and traffic is lighter than ever. The empty streets in the surrounding area contrast with the tumult at the station.

As she gets out of the car, the driver tries to stop the inevitable: Olga slams the door like people always do. He takes off quickly. Olga is resolved as she walks towards the spot where the different production trucks, curious onlookers and police cars have gathered. It's a hundred metres away. She's wearing low heels, and they're discreet, but they still click loudly in the thick and unusual silence. As Olga gets closer, the clicking of her steps blends into the noise coming from the station, forming a gradient of sound.

She tries not to look, but as she walks to where the cameras are, her eyes linger on the twisted pieces of metal sticking out behind the deserted platform. She pushes past the people, goes up to a young man she figures works for television, offers him a pastry and asks for permission to enter the small group around a cluster of arms holding up microphones and telephones. She plants herself behind a homeless person she recognizes because he lives at the station. He's telling the cameras, yet again, what happened at the moment of the accident. When the man appears to have finished his story, Olga elbows him aside slightly and faces the microphones and telephones:

"Someone is missing. My son-in-law is missing."

E VELYN'S COMMUNION PHOTO fills the whole screen. An index finger, which ends in a long nail painted Pearly Pink, points to Hugo's face. Pearly Pink and Milky Way are the colours Olga paints her nails. She does them herself. She has a steady hand, it hardly ever trembles. The pink is from this morning, yesterday they were Milky Way. Marta has tried to find a pattern to this behaviour of her mother's, the idea being to predict what Olga will do next. She is now standing tall in front of the microphones, holding a photograph, asking them to please look hard for Hugo Víctor Lamadrid, a labourer from Ituzaingó who was on the train. Marta gasps when the nail moves towards the image of her and Evelyn, and Olga's voice names them and says they were shocked to learn of the news on their way to Colón. Mónica flips through the channels and mutters something about the holy wounds ofourlordJesusChrist.

Olga learnt by watching: she leans her head towards the reporter asking her a question and then, looking straight ahead, she speaks to all the microphones at once, and to none of them in particular, to the whole country, the authorities concerned, the government. Evelyn is crying and asks why her grandmother had to put an old photo of her on television, and to make matters worse, one from her communion, when there are so many better ones on Instagram. Mónica says it's got to be the only photo Grandma Olga has of her father. In it, Hugo is smiling at the morning viewers, his white shirt tucked into his jeans, a narrow black tie around his neck, a glass of champagne raised, his hair short, bearing a faint resemblance to Al Pacino. Marta looks tired and tense in the photo. The two are hugging the daughter who's being honoured.

I look awful, Evelyn complains, and Marta thinks, so do I, but she doesn't say anything. Ten minutes later the channels already have two images cut from the same family moment: Hugo smiling in a close-up and an identical Hugo, at a slightly wider angle, hugging Evelyn. Marta has stopped listening but remains frozen in front of the kitchen television. Mónica comes in all worked up, looks at the screen and goes back out to answer the landline, which has begun to ring non-stop, as have their mobiles.

"They cut you out of the photo," she yells from the hall.

E L RIFLE SENDS a message to his producer and another
to The Group.

> Have you seen who was on the train?
>
> //

He's quick, no one else has said anything. The clueless among
them might not even know. The news is unbelievable. His
producer is going to buy the idea and the guys in The Group
definitely will as well. El Rifle feels euphoric and also like
he's been struck—somewhere between the two. Poor Hugo.
Only three guys in The Group have responded. A few left
after they last met up. It's just the losers that remain. But
that doesn't matter, these three are pretty good. El Rifle
controls how much he says before inviting them onto the
floor. Marina can go screw herself.

At Haedo Station, Olga places the memento from Evelyn's
communion back in its frame. She'd removed it so they
could take photos of the photo. The man from the production truck keeps her there, stretching the conversation out
as long as he can. Olga isn't in a rush either. She speaks
deliberately and firmly. Sandra Lagos observes her with a

make-up remover towelette in her hand. She turns to say something to Marina while she wipes away her make-up. Once again, one of her eyes is perfectly made up and the other is not. Her face looks like the Terminator's when he's more or less done for. Marina doesn't wait for Sandra to speak, she's ahead of the host.

"I'll go look for her."

OLGA'S VOICE coming from the television startles Beto. The image of Hugo holding a glass of champagne that fills the entire 132-centimetre screen is even more unsettling. His mouth open, the remote control balanced in his hand, which is going weak, and his legs failing to hold him up, Beto tries to determine whether this will work in his favour or against him. He wasn't expecting this of Olga, and he's terrified and excited at the same time. Intuitively, he goes over the possibilities still up in the air, seeing images that don't turn into a sustainable scenario. He can't decide what to think. But he thinks big. He sees himself dead. Taking a plane. Giving interviews on television. Travelling to Bolivia by boat. At the front lines of a protest. Cutting up another body. He even sees himself fucking Marta. The last of these images disturbs him, but what worries him most is figuring out what Olga expects of him.

"Would you look at that, man. And us bikers are always taking the blame." The guy with the helmet is still there. Either that or he left and came back. Or he's another client. Beto can't remember if the man paid for the helmet. He's no longer listening to him. He tries to simplify all his options so that there are just two: go home to see what

Hugo's doing and wait for news or go to the station and back up Olga's report. But he stays in the shop and turns up the volume to hear if the old lady sends him some message in code.

HUGO IS WALKING DOWN a street in Haedo and he doesn't feel well. The heat is blurring his vision, causing his legs to go weak. He has to move quickly with what he's borrowed: the clothes, the money, the transit pass, Beto's old ID card. His head is exploding and while he walks he repeats his home address, his date of birth, the names of the streets in the centre of Ituzaingó, the times table, to check if his brain is still working. He enters a taxi stand and asks to go to Liniers. He has no plan. Something that's inside him but seems disconnected from him is making all the decisions. This has been happening more and more often.

The man from the taxi stand is saying something Hugo doesn't understand and is pointing to a plastic chair. He does what he's told and sits down. Everything around him is out of focus. His mind switched off when he left Beto's place and the strong sun began to beat down on his back. He has to hold on, not let himself faint, walk to the taxi, and then to the bus, because now he's thinking he's going to take a bus. He lowers his head and presses his eyes with his thumb and index finger so the dizziness passes. Then he gives the few blokes waiting at the taxi stand with him a sidelong glance to see if he's drawing any attention. They're not even looking at him.

The mental fog suddenly dissipates. There's some stimulus that puts him on alert, though he can't tell what it is or where it's coming from. The blokes have turned on the TV, his taxi seems to have been forgotten. They move closer to watch, and he does too, to calm his nerves. The Hugo he's about to leave behind forever greets him with a raised glass of champagne. It's then he realizes it was Olga's voice that shook him out of his stupor.

Hugo understands the sign.

He takes three steps towards the door and goes out onto the pavement in a furtive movement that's a little overacted. He waits a few seconds, pulls Beto's Harley Davidson hat down to his eyes and almost breaks into a run as he distances himself from the taxi, dying of laughter he can't contain.

MARTA DOESN'T have a predictable mother like most people do. This leaves her little room for bold acts. On more than one occasion she would have liked to say to hell with the whole game, but Olga's always changing the pieces, even what they're playing. She's the one who deals the surprises, not her daughters. A mother like Olga can cause permanent paralysis. It's just Marta's brain that works—her body doesn't react. Mónica, on the other hand, is able to move in a state of shock. She answers all the calls, notes down the name and number of every journalist, and a message. Every so often she shouts from the living room, saying she can't believe the whole country got her phone number from one second to the next. Everyone wants to speak to Marta and see Evelyn. These people are pleasant at first and then aggressive when they say goodbye. Some offer a transfer to the capital and lodging close to the news station. Mónica comes and goes from the kitchen, considering options with her sister as though they were holiday packages. Marta says no to everything. The tacit family agreement is that Hugo is dead, but Olga and her daughters haven't agreed on what to do about it.

Marta's lucidity when it comes to reading quickly and carefully is inversely proportional to her ability to act. She was only able to make it as far as Colón because her evacuation plan had been maturing inside her for a long time. But after they fled, there was nothing. And now Olga and the ghost of Hugo want to drag her by force and bury her, like one of those river currents that every so often carries someone away. Who would have thought? Olga and Hugo pulling her in the same direction.

It hasn't been more than two hours since her mother burst onto the morning news and the phone started going off. Marta watches the growing number of missed calls and messages on WhatsApp: 251, 252, 253. There are even journalists at the door now. Mónica lowers the blinds facing the street and runs to the supermarket for provisions. Evelyn stays in the kitchen, watching the television. At least now they're showing photos she looks better in. Marta locks herself up in the bathroom, tries to use her mobile without having to answer the dozens of calls coming in. She calls the only number that occurs to her. The moment she hears a voice on the other end, she sees a drop of blood on the grey tile.

Evelyn.

DOMÍNGUEZ HALTS when he feels Hugo's phone vibrating in his trousers. He knew that someone would eventually call. When he saw the mess Olga was making on television, he left the office. He moved the car before Mancuso could find it and proceed to bust his balls. For half an hour, he's been driving aimlessly, listening to the radio, swearing at Olga out loud and waiting for something to happen. And it happens. He looks to see who it is before answering.

"Marta…"

Between Evelyn's blood and the voice she believes to be Hugo's, a knot forms in Marta's throat. But she speaks.

"You're a disaster."

"Marta…"

"No. Listen to me. Don't come looking for Evelyn, don't write to her on Facebook. I don't want to know what you did. Don't come here, don't get us involved, don't even think about showing up."

"Marta, this is Detective Domínguez."

"…"

"From the Morón Police Department."

"Sorry, I wanted to speak to my mother and…"

"This is Hugo's telephone, Marta."

"I don't understand. Are you with him? Has he been detained?"

"Does that mean you're not convinced he's dead?"

Unlike Marta, Domínguez is used to this kind of thing, so he hurries to speak before she can think. He wants to frighten her into returning to Buenos Aires and collaborating.

"What are you doing with Hugo's phone?" she asks.

"It was among the things found on the train."

"So then he's dead! That's what we've been saying, Domínguez. Don't make me and Evelyn go to Buenos Aires. My mother is already taking care of this."

"Why did you leave Buenos Aires? Were you hoping to meet up with your husband?"

"He's not my husband."

"He sent you a message last night at… hold on, don't hang up, I have it right here… After the accident, ma'am. A message that said 'yes' in response to one you sent that said 'you there?' And before that there's another that…"

"I know. I know what it says, you don't have to read it to me. Is it true that he killed someone?"

"Everything seems to indicate that…"

"Why did he do it?"

"That we don't know. Why don't you come to Buenos Aires so we can talk calmly?"

"Are you allowed to be using his phone?"

"I'm the detective in charge of the investigation, ma'am."

"Are you allowed to use it to interrogate me?"

"You called."

"But that was to speak to Hugo."

"So you believe he's dead but you want to speak to him?"

"Shouldn't the phone be in a little plastic bag like everything they find?"

"This is not a movie, Marta."

"You're pursuing this with me because you don't know what to do. He died in the accident and the police can't find him."

"Marta, it's still early to speak of…"

"And on top of that you're using his mobile? Is it legal to steal a dead person's mobile, Domínguez?"

"All right. Don't come for the time being. They're going to use Evelyn's toothbrush for the DNA test. With the mess your mother is making, the matter will be out of my hands. The news stations are already bringing Olga in. There are photos of your family all over the place. It's just a matter of time before they find you in Colón."

"Right."

"And what are you planning to do?"

"Look, if I have to ask the media for help to find my husband, I'll…"

"Marta, you fled after I was at your house."

"I came to see my sister."

"Decidedly opportune."

"Well, it's also very opportune that I called my husband and you answered."

"You're right about that."

"That leaves us both in a pretty bad position, doesn't it?"

"Not exactly. It's logical for you to be looking out for your daughter, and it's logical for me to have access to confiscated material. Let's calm down and try to get to the truth. What do you think?"

"Of course, Detective."

E VELYN IS TRYING hard to cry. She wants to cry. That would be the most normal reaction. But Evelyn isn't normal, because when a girl loses her father, the tears come on their own. Nothing is normal today. But the worst is over. By now everyone must know she's an orphan and not a fugitive. After all that's happened they're not going to keep after her for Miss Laura's mobile. Or her aunt's vibrator.

Once Martín told her that his sister lost her virginity with a vibrator. That's the way he said it: lost her virginity. And it was like her boyfriend didn't believe her and they fought and it ruined her life. Evelyn isn't afraid it will ruin her life but she is worried about getting an infection, because her grandma says that if you stick things in there, you can get an infection. Now Evelyn is going to have to live with two secrets: having Miss Laura's mobile and losing her virginity.

But the worst is that she can't cry. The tears are going to have to come, because sometimes everyone looks at you, and they expect you to cry, and wonder: Why isn't she crying if her dad died? If he was in the train crash and no one saved him? If he was hurt really badly? And he yelled and called for help. And they couldn't save him. Or he was completely squashed. Or paralysed. No, he wasn't paralysed because he died first. He died before the pain. He died of suffocation. Or he lost a leg and couldn't bear it. Or he was struck hard in the head, and it was a concussion. Or his bones broke. But he didn't feel a thing, because when something terrible happens to you, you don't feel a thing. He yelled and called for help. Or he helped the other people and then fainted. But they can't find him. Because a body is missing, her grandma said. And they have to look for him. But Evelyn doesn't feel a thing. She just doesn't.

THE DEAD don't take the bus. That's the first thing that pops into Hugo's head when he sits down on the 57 bus. Let Uzquiaga say that to him now. And let the others laugh, the bright kids. Rafael Uzquiaga, founding father of photojournalism, hero of intellectual honesty, the King of Dignity—that's what they'd nicknamed him in English—and the professor who'd stamped a label on Hugo, saying, "Do something else for a living, this isn't for you." Uzquiaga had been irate, offended, invested with a moral weariness after all the times he'd had to explain to Hugo what he hadn't understood: the dead don't take the bus.

The casualties were travelling in car seven on line four. Hugo still repeats this sentence when someone asks him why he left journalism school. Because he didn't learn that the dead don't take the bus and other truths. He talks to Uzquiaga in his head, as though his old professor could hear him, respond to him.

"Not much happened in my life, but same goes for yours."

Uzquiaga was never the director of a newspaper or university, no one paid homage to him, and he never got rich. One of his former students published the news of his death on Facebook—he'd died fairly poor in a state geriatric home. The successful students collected money to help him on a few occasions, but the last time El Rifle organized the fundraiser, no one donated anything. El Rifle embraced the cause of Uzquiaga's decline and passing as though the professor were his father. He visited the old man, talked to the doctors, showed up with former students so Uzquiaga could tell the same anecdotes as always. It was likely that El Rifle didn't care much about Uzquiaga, but through his devotion to the man, was able to imprint in other students' minds memories they didn't have. For example, that he'd been one of Uzquiaga's favourites, or even that he wrote well. El Rifle Barrios is a brute. He always has been.

Hugo lets his aching body decide what to do: when to get off the 57 bus and start walking. He dozes a little in the heat of the sun coming through the window, looking at the monotonous landscape of the highway, grass and stands that sell things to people in gated communities. He smiles thinking about The Group, which is what they still call it. He's getting his revenge. Every so often they include him when they have a barbecue. They've got to be sending each other messages now, bits of memories. They're going to have to talk about him, write about him. They won't be such arseholes as to mention the casualties. One of them might even make the same mistake that resulted in Hugo's nickname Huguito: the victim took the Sarmiento railway line. What does it matter anyway. He almost wants to turn himself in just so El Rifle Barrios and the ghost of Uzquiaga will shut their traps. To prove the dead do take the bus.

No one is looking at him on the 57 bus, which is taking him out of the city. Hugo has already forgotten why he's on it and where he's going. He's not thinking about Marta or about his daughter. Only about Uzquiaga and The Group. Everything that happened between car seven on line four crashing into a truck on the Costanera Sur and the train accident at Haedo Station is parenthetical: giving up on his ambitions, getting married, failing, becoming a father, getting depressed, getting better, accepting things, complicating things, killing someone, hiding it, fleeing and staying alive like a dead person who takes the bus.

PART THREE

T HE GRILLE FITS the Christ perfectly. The iron bars are attached to a small aquamarine wall that also supports his afflicted feet. The bars have pointed ends that are like lances behind the head crowned in thorns. Jesus and the grille are the same height. Before the people and television crews arrived, Mónica moved the swan with impatiens in it from the entrance to the back patio so the Christ would get all the attention. In front of her humble home in Colón, everything is now pain, thorns, nails and a grille with spikes. Some teenage boys unload grapefruit soda and white-bread sandwiches from a van with an ad for the casino printed on it. The news channels are talking to the neighbours. They know Mónica because she lives here, the girl and her mother because they visit during the summer. "It is not known whether the authorities have spoken to the women. Official silence, then, while the prayer chain begins at exactly two in the afternoon, disrupting the habitual siesta and calm in this town in the country's interior," says the young man from Sandra Lagos's production truck, facing the camera and the sun. Mónica is waiting next to him, blushing and fanning herself with some papers.

The Christ crucified on the grille doesn't look like any of those Evelyn has seen before. There's a lot of really dark blood dripping down his face, chest and legs, like thick threads of brown glue. The huge nails go through his hands and his flesh has opened up and ripped from the weight of his hanging body. He's in penury, this Christ. He's not the normal Jesus everyone knows about. Her aunt got mad when she said so and that's why she won't let Evelyn go on television. She's not allowed to leave the house, use the tablet or answer the phone. They also moved her from the room with the window facing the street. She can go to the kitchen, the bathroom and the other bedroom, where she spent the night with her mum and aunt, listening to the journalists ring the doorbell and the two of them arguing.

"You're going to have to answer, Marta. But don't tell them about Hugo's problems."

"Then what am I going to tell them, Mónica?"

"Mum, what problems?"

"You don't have to tell them anything, Marta. They just want to talk to you. It's an opportunity."

"An opportunity for what?"

"An opportunity, Marta! I don't know what for!"

Evelyn can handle being stuck indoors now, and also the uncertainty, and the pinching between her legs. It's the price for saving herself and her dad. She's not going to eat until she's skin and bones like the Christ on the grille. She savours the pain of penitence. She doesn't want it to go away, but to feel it in all its intensity. What Evelyn wants is to feel. With the fury of a saint. And to be strong for what's to come, whether it's prison or ending up an orphan. She walks barefoot in the half-light, trying to become invisible, to hide the euphoria of feeling like a martyr. Her mum's silence isn't that bad. It means they won't have to talk about things, like what to do about the police and what happened with the vibrator. Her mum doesn't want to be on television so that her dad turns up sooner. Evelyn is dying to know what everyone is saying.

The TV screen in the kitchen is playing back what's happening in front of the house. More and more people are arriving. There are four channels from the capital and one from Colón. But now no one is ringing the doorbell, because ever since her aunt organized the prayer chain, there have been two rows of women—Mónica's friends, sex-toy clients and colleagues—seated on plastic stools in front of the house. To reach the door, the journalists would have to jump over the women and climb the grille; they prefer to stay put and chat. Not much of the racket outside reaches the kitchen. It's just a murmur with the television on mute. On the screen, everything is a lot noisier and more animated.

Evelyn is waiting for her chance to be on TV like an actress backstage on a set. She got around surveillance twice and spied through the gaps in the blinds that face the front. But she couldn't see anything. Only silhouettes against the light. Only the backs of Jesus and her aunt's friends seated on the pavement, some candles and cards, and flowers attached to the grille's bars. Everything was facing away from her.

On the full HD screen, the sun hits the Christ on the grille head-on and enhances his colours. The blood now appears more red than brown and even looks like it's spurting live and direct from the deep wound in his right torso. How Jesus was wounded in this part of his body, where there are no nails or thorns, is a mystery. Evelyn looks for an answer in a leaflet she found under the bed, a guide to all the wounds, each with an explanation. Her aunt had stored it with the Christ next to a box full of vibrators and related items she'd wanted to hide. But luck was not on her side, because when she took out the crucified Jesus, the blanket she'd wrapped the items in dragged them across the floor.

"Mum, what does 'with my wounds and my divine heart, everything can be obtained' mean?"

Evelyn can't bear her vow of silence any longer, there are things she needs to ask. But Marta isn't answering because Mónica now has her attention on each of the five news channels, where she appears with an A4-size printout of a photo of Hugo hanging from her neck, a rosary in her right hand and a megaphone in her left.

"My Jesus, during present dangers, cover us with your precious blood," Mónica orates and everyone follows her in chorus, reading the photocopied lines that exalt the wounds.

Sandra Lagos can't help but feel disgusted and disconcerted. Her gaze is fixed on the monitor showing images of Mónica praying, direct from Colón. Out of the corner of her eye, she's barely glancing at Olga, who's trying to get comfortable on the edge of a prop armchair while a producer arranges a pillow under her bum so she sits upright.

"She likes this rosary more than the usual one. I don't know why," Olga tells her, so she has something to say. But she can't explain further because they signal for her to be quiet. They're about to go on air.

In a second, Sandra Lagos directs all of her body language towards Olga, places a hand on her knee and with her peripheral vision, confirms the camera's red light is on.

"You were telling me, Olga, that your daughter is very religious…"

A few metres away, in the control room, where the monitors are reproducing Sandra Lagos's contained emotion and Olga's integrity from several angles, the programme director lets out the air he's been holding in his lungs for the last ten seconds. He knows that Sandra Lagos is going to take the conversation from faith to solidarity and from solidarity to inaction and the lack of response on the part of the authorities. She'll need a minimum of fifteen minutes to do this, as well as to talk to Colón and get things on track. He leaves the control room in large strides, the call under way.

"Marina, sweetie, listen to me, any chance you have another Christ we can use?"

Olga's gaze is fixed on the camera as she speaks directly into the eyes of the whole country. And in Mónica's kitchen in Colón, Marta feels her mother's eyes are fixed on her as well, to the point of pulverizing her. She feels immobilized just like those parasites that grow around a trunk until they become the tree themselves. Marta knows her mother is a torrent capable of bringing her down as easily as a dry branch is carried away by a river. That's why she prefers to stay put on the shore. But Olga still finds a way to drag her downstream.

"I thirst for souuuls!"

Evelyn shouts this in a trance as she walks around the kitchen with her arms outstretched like in one of those zombie movies, startling Marta.

"Lower your voice, Evelyn, what are you doing? They'll hear us outside."

"Jesus said this to a virgin." Evelyn shows her mother the leaflet of the rosary of the holy wounds.

"I offer you the wounds ofourlordJesusChrist to heal the wounds of our souls!" Mónica repeats, the sun in her eyes, her natural blonde curls slightly stuck to her forehead with sweat, before handing the megaphone to one of her colleagues, because Marina, the young woman from Sandra Lagos's programme, has managed to get her away from the competition's cameras and is leading her to the corner.

"Mónica, I wanted to ask you if you'll be reciting a rosary shortly."

"We are reciting a rosary, dear."

"I know, I know, I was wondering if you would recite one more… less… something more… heartening, positive."

"I don't understand."

"In a moment, when Sandra Lagos has finished talking to your mother, we're going to focus on you, on all these people praying, I mean. Wouldn't you like to say a Hail Mary, because it's better... known?"

"Do you think? The thing is we've already made the photocopies."

"We want to help, Mónica, to show that people have really come together here for Hugo. But all of the channels are showing images of the accident, of the bodies. You already know this."

"It's dreadful—why show all that blood instead of helping?"

"That's why I'm telling you that... the part about the wounds seems a little strong. People have been sensitized, and it may cause them to... reject your family's cause. The exact opposite of what we want, Mónica."

"Of course."

"I don't want to worry you any more, but some of the outlets are already saying that your sister bought the bus tickets after the crash."

"Why are they saying that?"

"Because they requested the information from the bus company."

"And what's wrong with that?"

"They're saying that it's... strange that she left like that. The thing is they're official channels, instead of investigating what the government..."

"And so you're saying that I start just like that, with a Hail Mary? Will you tell me when?"

M ancuso's fingers tap the image of St Expeditus, as the department head shifts his gaze between the three men he's talking to. The head of operations at Haedo Station has his back against the window, his arms crossed. He was a hero yesterday morning, but in the last twenty-four hours he's become a good-for-nothing who can't explain what happened to the body of Hugo Víctor Lamadrid. In the centre of the room, a firefighter sergeant, Marcelo, is shifting his weight back and forth, between the balls of his feet and his heels, while he opens and closes his fists. Domínguez is leaning against the door frame, facing the hallway, focused on the yoghurt Ramírez brought him for his heartburn. Mancuso finally speaks.

"So whose shitshow is this?"

The department head is the only one who's seated. Behind him, on a very large television screen, Olga is talking to the head of operations, looking him directly in the eye, asking him why he hasn't helped her or given her an explanation, demanding that he tell her whom he answers to and why he won't say what happened to Hugovíctor's body. That's what Sandra Lagos has been calling him, Hugovíctor, his first and middle names stuck together without his last name. And now that's what the whole country is calling him.

"She never asked me, she went straight to the TV channels," the head of operations clarifies to Mancuso.

"I have a friend at that channel, we can let them know…" the sergeant cuts in. He doesn't finish his sentence because Domínguez lets out a sharp cry.

A liquid that's red and viscous, like the blood of Mónica's Christ on the grille, is spreading along the office's parquet flooring. Domínguez's plastic spoon is suspended in the air, his movement interrupted by disgust.

"What's in this? Ramírez!" he yells towards the other office. "What did you get me?"

"Let's calm down a little," Mancuso yells even louder, though he's not calm at all. He's spinning his Bersa like a roulette wheel on his desk, which results in more nervous oscillations on the part of the sergeant, who was summoned to the head chief's dispatch after the latter arrived at his station in the morning and learned that Hugovíctor had come out of the train alive.

"There's some important information about Lamadrid that you may not be aware of," Domínguez says, taking the floor as he stirs the thick red substance at the bottom of the yoghurt. Mancuso doesn't let him finish.

"It's a fruit base, you idiot. When's the last time you bought yoghurt? They all come like that now."

Domínguez understands he's talking too much. He goes into the hall, tosses the container of yoghurt into a bin two metres away and turns back to Mancuso, his hands raised like he's holding up a tray, indicating that the department head is free to speak. The yoghurt bounces off the edge of the bin and falls to the floor. Mancuso doesn't resume the conversation because he wants to continue watching Sandra Lagos's channel.

There's a heart in the centre of the screen. A red heart and a fire giving off rays of light. A heart in flames that moves into the distance, growing smaller in the centre of the image, while its luminous flashes linger in the bright white tunic that covers Jesus from his neck to his ankles. His serene face appears, with no trace of suffering, between the afternoon sun's rays and those emanating from his very presence. The index finger of his right hand is pointing slightly upwards and forwards, a baby lamb is resting its head on his left palm, his straight hair is perfect and frizz-free up to his ears, at which point it falls in a loose wave that cascades onto his white tunic, which merges with more flashes and thornless roses and doves, all the same shade of white on a vinyl tarp that shines in front of Mónica's house, the cradle of Hugovíctor, live from Colón. Mancuso raises the volume to listen to Mónica's Hail Mary, while over her voice, the pastor, who brought the tarp, yells something about a lost lamb, and the cameraman, who has quick reflexes, zooms in on the little animal on Jesus's forearm.

"What did you say your name was?" Mancuso asks, as he rotates his office chair and returns to the conversation.

Marcelo says Marcelo for the fourth time since he arrived at the office. It's not that the department head has a problem with names, but that he's putting each of them in their place in the conversation. He goes back to tapping his thick fingers on the wrinkled St Expeditus holy card. The fire-fighter sergeant brought it as proof that his story was true. Mancuso rotates towards the television, and for a moment he watches the luminous Jesus that's replaced the Christ on the grille. Then he returns to the squat saint's worn little figure. A jack of cups in the Spanish deck.

"Do you know who St Expeditus was?"

"He's a very popular saint, sir."

"A bloke who was too anxious. Is who he *was*."

Marcelo starts swaying again. He looks to the head of operations for help. The man is passing *mate* to Mancuso and pretends not to see him. Domínguez is still in the door frame with his arms crossed, staring vacantly into the hallway. The department head picks up where he left off:

"This fellow, Expeditus, was a Roman soldier. That's why he's dressed the way he is, in his little skirt. He worked for them. But what happens is that one day he has a revelation or something like that, and he wants to convert to Christianity. The Romans, as you can imagine, want to destroy him. But the bloke still wants to convert. Because he's convinced of his beliefs, his truth, you understand? And he makes haste. He doesn't want to think it over a little, wait for everything to calm down. No. And when he's converting, he sees a raven that cries out to him: 'Tomoooorrow, leave it for tomoooorrow.' But Expeditus doesn't listen, he stamps on the raven, killing it, because he wants to convert today, right now. He can't wait. The bloke feels his truth is burning him from the inside. So he converts. And becomes a saint. That's why he's the patron saint of urgent matters, of things that can't wait. But the Romans killed him just the same."

Mancuso pauses dramatically, as though he's waiting for the conclusions to spill into his dispatch under their own weight, and then returns to his initial question:

"Whose shitshow is this then?"

He puts the holy card in his shirt pocket and gets up to indicate the conversation is over. He approaches the head of operations, places his hands on the man's shoulders, first patting him and then grabbing hold of him tightly.

"No need to be anxious. We need to be sure first. If this young man is right, the shitshow is theirs. You got Hugovíctor out and handed him over to the paramedics. From that moment on, the body is not yours. From the platform on, it's their problem. Don't worry. Keep your cool."

T HE BEATLES Pappo The Rolling Stones the sky The
Beatles Pappo The Rolling Stones the sky The Beatles
Pappo The Rolling Stones the sky the sky the sky the sky
the sky. Hugo bounces a few times, his eyes on the sky, his
arms open in a cross, his head back, until the ride machinery
starts rotating again, this time in the opposite direction. The
Rolling Stones Pappo The Beatles the sky The Rolling Stones
Pappo The Beatles the sky The Rolling Stones Pappo The
Beatles the sky the sky the sky the sky. The machine bounces
when Hugo's looking at the sky again. The music playing
has nothing to do with The Beatles, The Rolling Stones or
the musician Pappo. Hugo thinks it's cumbia, everything
sounds like cumbia these days, but it's not. It goes something
like cha cha cha pum chacha real quick and strikes his back
against the hard, rough seat, bouncing him with increasing
force until he feels like he's going to fly off. Then it stops.

He looks around for Spot, but hears a sound like tututu
tututu pipipipipipipipipipipipipiiiiiii and then the machine starts
again abruptly. It shakes and creaks like scrap metal, a sound
that reminds Hugo of the carriage warping. He wants to get
off. His body is being whipped around at a rhythm that's
like a batucada, he realizes, now that someone is singing in

Brazilian. It's insane, it goes bum bum and tam tam and causes his legs to fly up above the seat. All of his muscles hurt from being fastened into it like someone on a cross. He yells "stop stop stop" but no one hears him. His hands come loose. He'd wanted to get up and bow down to Pappo, balancing, walking on the spot in the opposite direction to the machine's rotation, but he doesn't manage it. He ends up rolling around on the floor, first in one direction, then the other, until he grabs hold of an ankle, which belongs to one of the four kids who got on with him. The kid kicks, trying to shake Hugo off so he's not dragged down, at which point the machine begins to reduce its revolutions. The Samba ride moves slower and slower until it stops, descends as though it were a flying saucer and lets out a sound like a bellows deflating. Spot is waiting for him calmly under a small tree. Rati and Rottweiler are a little further off, staring at one of the Super 8 cars that's climbing slowly. Hugo wants to run over to watch it. The Super 8 used to be the second biggest rollercoaster. The only one that topped it was the Super Tornado. But he's dizzy and can't feel his arms. He's still standing, stumbling a little, in the centre of the tin circle that now seems inoffensive. The girl with blue hair who was operating the chairlift yesterday is waiting for him to get off so she can lock the door. Hugo asks her what music she'd put on and if the ride is really the same Samba as the one at Italpark. She hasn't heard of that amusement park and Hugo will never be able to repeat the name she tells him, but he's sure it's Brazilian.

"Then why do they have drawings of the Beatles and the Rolling Stones? Do you even know who Pappo was?"

Blue Hair shrugs her shoulders and Hugo stays put for a few seconds, holding on to the banister and looking at the painted portraits on a triptych of sheet metal that makes up the rest of the Samba's set. They're really warped. He recognizes the Beatles by their fringes, Keith by his head scarf, and Pappo because he's Pappo. The portraits don't make any sense. They're there, though anything else could have been, to cover up the sad sight of what's behind them.

Rati and Rottweiler run back and forth along the wire fence that separates them from the Super 8. They grow desperate when the car goes by with some secondary-school girls shouting with fear and excitement, and they bark as though they could smell meat. But Spot goes up to Hugo and licks his hand. Slowly, they cross the bridge over the dead water called a river, to the bank where there's a basilica and rollercoaster that's less roundabout, which goes for its name as well: it's called Rollercoaster. The music playing on the loudspeaker really is cumbia now. Hugo has three chips in his pocket but his arms are still shaking, so he walks away from the rides towards the seven o'clock mass. The evening sun is horizontal and lights up the gargoyles more than it does the saints and apostles. Spot stays at the door, he doesn't enter the church.

Inside, no one is praying for Hugovíctor. Each of the worshippers is there for their own reason—they're all praying for illnesses and other shitty things. Hugo has a photo of himself from the newspaper, a red ribbon with an image of the virgin on it and another of St Expeditus. He wasn't sure which ribbon to buy: "protect my business", "protect my trip" or "protect my family". In the end, he decided on the trip ribbon. There's a line at the confessional, so he pets Greyhound's back and leaves. In the City of Luján, only the dogs recognize him.

There's almost no one around, but at the parrilla restaurants, they're still tossing fat onto the grill so it'll smoke. Hugo plans to go back to the place he was at last night, because they had El Rifle Barrios's programme on and also because it's next to the shop that stamps T-shirts with a photo of you in the basilica. He plans to have a T-shirt made with his photo and have it say SUCK MY DICK, RIFLE, for when they find him.

Hugo watches the last of the sun's rays drop behind a tree before he free-falls on the Rollercoaster. Marta never wanted to join him, she never had the courage to rise high with him. To let herself fall. To experience the vertigo. He doesn't miss Marta at all.

B ETO TRIES OUT the armchair he bought with the last of his earnings from Olga. He adjusts the leg support and reclines too far back. He has to fix the angle so he can see the TV screen and eat pizza at the same time. In the act, he knocks over his bottle of beer. Things are not going well. It's the first time in a month he's been able to rest his head for more than two hours in a row. Though night is falling, he keeps the blinds closed. The oversized screen turns his face blue, his anxious movements too. He swears under his breath, then a little louder and finally he's practically yelling. He gets up, slamming his hands into the armrests, kicks the bathroom door open and pisses without turning on the light. On his way back, he punches the wall in the hallway a few times.

He checks his phone, tosses it onto the end table where his pizza is getting cold, then stands there for a while with his hands at his waist, looking at the television. It's all gone wrong. He'd been making a career for himself as a player in Europe. But then he went and fucked up a few times because the piece-of-shit controller isn't responsive.

He shoves the fridge door shut, knocking over everything inside. Then he returns to the armchair with another beer.

The match and the swearing begin again. His team is playing Bayer Leverkusen. This is his chance. He has to stop thinking about WhatsApp. Now is not the time. Twenty-four hours have passed since he decided to lower the blinds at the shop, barricade himself at home with his PlayStation and wait for something to happen. But nothing is happening out there, except that Olga's on television.

No one can find Hugovíctor, victim and murderer. And the guy who knows everything about both Hugovíctors is holed up in his living room, trying to get from the last sixteen to the finals in the Champions League. No one knows he exists. He hasn't received a single call or visit from a police officer or journalist. No one has put him at the scene, so he's not there. Beto is no one. He's the only spectator watching himself in his role as protagonist. It's the best thing that could happen to him. He knows this, but it bugs him a little. He's not responsible for his anonymity, because it depends on what his friend and his boss want to do, and this frustrates him a lot. He loses in the last minute and swings the controller around. When your thoughts move quickly and you're able to read the play but can't act at the same speed, when your movements are slower than your mind, you lose. It's what's happening to him with Olga and Hugo—he can't control the game. He doesn't make it to the Champions League finals.

He gets up with the full force of his anger and crushes Hugo's controller under his sneaker. He's not sure whether to throw it out or not, because he'd personalized it for Hugo on Friendship Day. It was a gift. He's also unsure whether

Hugo is still his friend. Things always end badly when they play FIFA. Hugo says he's immature, that no one acts the way he does because of PlayStation, that it's a game—not a match, not reality. And Beto yells that everyone acts the way they want and that the game is just as realistic as a real match. Because if you get into the game and play it, who can say if it's real or not?

EL RIFLE WANTS all the shine to be removed from his skin. And he won't wear brown shoes. He hates brown shoes. He goes through the notifications on his phone, scrolling up and down. He has to think of something for today's programme and has no idea what. His mobile doesn't have the answer. The lady from wardrobe, who insisted that brown shoes would go better with a blue suit, has now run off, her eyes full of tears, to look urgently for black trousers. El Rifle is in socks, walking among the cables behind the set. Today of all days, with everything that's going on, they had to tell him it would be better to do the programme standing up instead of seated. He's about to enter the studio for an hour-long struggle with two MPs from the opposition. With brown shoes on, he won't be in the mood to greet them or go ahead with any of it. No one's come up with a better option than the MPs. Not a civil servant, or a family member, or a survivor. To make matters worse, Sandra Lagos has Olga, and Marta isn't answering her phone. Marta's been very ungrateful, truth be told. The bosses were hoping for something better after yesterday's programme.

As soon as the bomb fell—that a body was missing—El Rifle started a WhatsApp chat for The Group of graduates, only without Hugo, and yesterday night's programme spared nothing. He had photos no one else did and journalist friends telling stories as both interviewees and panellists. Everyone at the channel was pleased. And the members of The Group too, because El Rifle is the only one of them who doesn't have a shit job. This time they were able to help. El Rifle got them a bit of exposure and not one has responded with a message or information.

It looked like the push El Rifle had been needing for the channel to take him a bit more seriously. But today he's at as much of a loss as everyone else. He goes through the calendar on his phone to see if there's a name that stands out and gives him something to go on. It's all press officers and football players. He leaves the studio swearing and comes back in with brown shoes on. Then he greets the MPs and looks at his phone one last time, repeating a nervous habit, which involves moving his thumb over the WhatsApp messages that appear at full speed before his eyes, like the wheel on a slot machine. Only instead of cherries and number sevens, it's names that are of no use: his trainer, two birds, the producer, brands sending him invitations for things, his ex, Huguito, the guys, his mum, the other producer. Wait, he says to himself. He goes back. Huguito. Of course. What an idiot. He opens his chat with Hugo from before the last barbecue and above it, he reads, "last seen yesterday at 2:22 p.m." It's crystal clear. Oh, shit, he thinks. And then they're on air.

SOMETHING DARK and thick spurts from the meat where it's been cut. It's as though pieces of the Christ on the grille, surrounded by potatoes noisette, were shining beneath the microwave's artificial light instead of Evelyn's dinner. She's feeling nauseated. She doesn't want her food. Her aunt offers her the vegetarian option: four-cheese ravioli with butternut squash. The casino sent them tomorrow's menu. Tomorrow's a Thursday, ladies' night, and her aunt has to go to work no matter what because things get very busy and she's already had two days off.

"You're going to have to take over the door, Marta."

Evelyn moves the raviolis around on her plate until they get cold. Then she gets up from the table and leaves the kitchen. They don't try to keep her there or reproach her for not having eaten anything because they're arguing.

Evelyn's mum doesn't want to have anything to do with the prayer chain or the journalists, nor does she want to call Grandma Olga. They're talking about her a lot. And saying nothing about her dad. From the part of the house that's off limits, she hears the muffled hum from the street. Evelyn ventures along the hallway, a few steps further than the imaginary line she's not allowed to cross between the bathroom and "study" doors. She goes that far to breathe a bit of the fresh air entering from the living room. They've been cooped up for two days now, and it's likely she won't be able to handle another. This part of being famous is awful. And it's the only part she's experienced.

In the kitchen, her mum and aunt fall silent because someone is saying Evelyn's name on TV. It's the famous journalist who's a friend of her dad's. El Rifle Barrios is angry and says that Evelyn deserves to know the truth. Or maybe it's not that he's angry, it's just that her mum and aunt have turned up the volume on the television again.

O LGA IS ASLEEP keeling over in the armchair in front of the television. The MPs on El Rifle's programme are shouting and calling for heads to roll but they don't wake her. The doorbell does. If it's Sandra Lagos's channel again, she's going to have to set limits. The day got off to a good start but then things became tense and she had to ask them to respect her family's privacy. You've got to be grateful, but you can't go on being part of the media show, Olga had to tell them, and all because Marta packed up and left. Olga knows Sandra Lagos really is kind and that she understands what Hugovíctor's wife and daughter are going through. The host just wants to ask Marta why she left for Colón a few hours after the tragedy occurred, why she didn't stay in Buenos Aires. Since Hugo hasn't shown up, they're ready to fill airtime with anything. When Marta left should have nothing to do with it. The only thing that matters to them is their ratings.

The doorbell rings again right as Olga is spying through the peephole. Mancuso is talking in the space between the door and the frame. He introduces himself, giving his first and last name, and his position, and he waits.

El Rifle looks at the camera and says he has a question that could change everything.

THE PRAYER CHAIN has its own biorhythm. The voice praying on the megaphone, the sandwiches, the people and cool drinks are regularly renewed without the decision being centrally organized by anyone. It's that life is simpler outside the capital, Marina philosophizes while she sits in Sandra Lagos's production truck, waiting for Mónica to send news from inside the house. She's listening to El Rifle's programme without watching it and sending WhatsApp messages to a friend, saying she has proof the host should be called "the North Korean missile" instead of "the rifle". At this time of day no one is broadcasting, but the reporters from four national channels and one local station are ready in case they need to go on air, the cameras in their tripods, spotlights illuminating Jesus, so he's even brighter against his tarp. The people praying, eating and talking about the news don't have much of an idea when they're on television and when they're not. Marina sends another WhatsApp message.

> Though El Rifle doesn't really know
> what to do with what he's got.
>
> ✓✓

The circle of Mónica's friends is preventing access to what everyone now calls Marta's bunker. Behind them are the cameras, and a little further back the organized group of people praying, nosy onlookers, and a periphery of messengers for other causes, who are rallying people to pray for the girl who needs a transplant, and the boy who took his boat out on the river and never came back. A few metres from the epicentre, Evelyn is spying through the slats in the blinds. She's still waiting to enter the scene, to be where the blaze of light is coming from, and also the voice offering the wounds ofourlordJesusChrist to heal our souls' wounds. Only she can't see any of it because Jesus's tarp is covering everything.

Mónica negotiated with Sandra Lagos's producer for two hours of the rosary of the holy wounds outside of primetime in exchange for an attempt at getting her sister to break her silence.

"It's not my fault, Marta, Mum was the one who started it. You should be glad management is my thing and I was able to organize all this." Mónica is getting mad. She can't handle the pressure any longer and needs Marta to do something.

El Rifle calls for attention. He does so in a way that causes even Mónica to fall silent. He looks at the camera and asks what happened to Hugovíctor's mobile phone. It's not clear whom he's speaking to—not even El Rifle knows. But he does know that Hugovíctor's mobile was used yesterday at around 2:22 p.m.

Confirmed: El Rifle never knows
what to do with what he's got.

✓/

MARINA SENDS this last message to her friend and heads straight from the production truck to the door of Marta's bunker.

"El Rifle is such an idiot," Hugo says, his voice loud enough for those nearby to hear him.

In the end, the parrilla began to fill up, and now half the tables are occupied. Mostly with men eating on their own. Hugo isn't out of place, except for the fact that he feels like chatting. He waits for his neighbour to respond, but the bloke is dividing his attention between the television and the chitterlings on his plate. So Hugo goes up to him and continues.

"You know what? If you say 'around 2:00' that's fine, but 'around 2:22' makes no sense, because 2:22 is the exact time, it's not around anything—see what I'm saying?"

What Hugo has never been able to comprehend is why El Rifle made it and he didn't.

"SO THEN THERE'S HOPE?"

Olga and Mancuso are listening to El Rifle's revelation. The news surprised them mid-introductions—they hadn't even had a chance to sit down. Olga asks her question in a tone that reflects neither hope nor surprise. Mancuso doesn't like the news either, but he hides it better. He sits down in an armchair, his whole body leaning towards Olga. He motions for her to make herself comfortable in front of him. He fixes his eyes on her, something Mancuso does well, like an animal that looks at you from below but is really calculating how far it will have to jump to reach you.

"You must care a good deal for your son-in-law…"

Olga presses her lips together before opening her mouth to speak. But the department head doesn't give her time to fire off a stream of clichés to the effect of her obviously caring for Evelyn's father.

"…because boy will you become a laughing stock if it turns out you created a scandal for a martyr who is in fact alive and what's more is a criminal…"

"I don't follow."

Mancuso relaxes now, leans back against the armchair,

undoes the button on his jacket, crosses his legs and looks at the ceiling.

"Ma'am, I'm aware of what Detective Domínguez does. The police force is a top-down institution."

HUGO LINGERS outside the parrilla for a while. He has a bottle of whisky in his hand. There's another bottle in his backpack, along with a litre of holy water in a plastic container. He's watching the TV through the window but can no longer hear what El Rifle and the others are saying. It's a clear night and the moon is almost full beyond the clock on the church's left tower. The time is two minutes behind what it says on television.

"How is it that the church isn't synchronized with official time?" Hugo asks into the air.

Spot looks at him, thinks Hugo is talking to him or that he's going to give him a bone. The clock on the other tower isn't even working. Nothing's working right.

Hugo takes a swig from the bottle and walks slowly, dragging his feet. Greyhound comes over to him. The dog spends the night outdoors, he's kicked out of the confessional at closing time. The three of them cross the emptiness that's neither a square nor a street, their backs to the basilica, like pilgrims that made it this far only to confirm that God doesn't exist, or that God does exist but has abandoned them, and now they have to go back tired and without hope.

El Rifle has no clue what he's doing. "Because maybe the victim didn't take the train," he said. It's enough to drive you mad. It turns out that now El Rifle believes the dead can take transport. And even talk on the phone. More and more people agree on this. Everyone but that old piece of shit Uzquiaga. In the end Hugo wasn't wrong. That or his mistake wasn't a big deal. But it's too late now, there's less and less time left. To change nothing. To down the whisky, first on its own, then with some holy water, always fifty-fifty. To help time pass quicker. Because Uzquiaga is no longer around to correct him, to come and tell him that hours are neither long nor short, that they always last the same amount of time. Though that all depends. They'd have to ask Uzquiaga whether dying seemed to last a long time. Hugo laughs a little and Spot doesn't understand why.

"Better yet I'll have a shirt made that says THE DEAD TAKE THE BUS," Hugo tells the dogs and sits down on the kerb of the main street to fill half a plastic cup with whisky, half with holy water.

Spot perks up his ears, looks towards the end of the street and takes off running. Hugo also wants to look but he's stunned by a light coming straight at him and the sound of motorcycles that seem to have appeared out of nowhere. The first runs over the cup. The bloke riding the second knocks him over with a kick. It all lasts an instant. Hugo sees Greyhound lapping up the puddle of whisky and the bottle still rolling a few metres from him. He lies there looking at the sky. And then he begins to cry and says Evelyn's name.

DOMÍNGUEZ IS EATING a roasted chicken breast off a plastic tray. Ramírez picked it up for him at the deli. On his desk are two mobile phones. One has a message from Mancuso ordering Domínguez to stay late and stop by his office. The other is Hugo's and it's ringing. On Wednesdays, Ramírez has Domínguez on a diet, and that's the day he feels most anxious and miserable. If he has to wait until some ridiculous hour for the department head, and the topic of conversation is going to be Hugovíctor's mobile phone, he's going to have to order dessert.

Domínguez needs something sweet to dissolve his bitter Wednesday thoughts, the kind you have as an adult, when you're tired and there's some setback, like your boss wanting to ask you about a mobile phone, because he suspects that a detail like this couldn't have gotten past an intelligent bloke like yourself. Domínguez puts the device on silent and places it back in the right pocket of his trousers. Ramírez has left, so he buys himself a triple *alfajor* cookie from the vending machine in the hallway, while in his head he puts a response in order that doesn't include the words "intuition" and "curiosity". He already knows what Mancuso is going to say: this needs to be solved.

Thirty years as an investigator and his status as a legend isn't enough. The abyss is there, separating him from those around him, beginning with the department head. What matters today isn't knowing the truth. It's resolving a case that counts.

M ónica's world is falling apart.
      "He's using his phone. He's crazy. If he turns out to be alive, they're going to kill me here."

Sandra Lagos's producer doesn't like the news about Hugovíctor's mobile either. She's at Mónica's front door, having dodged her circle of friends, and is alternating between pressing down on the bell and sending WhatsApp messages. Inside, Mónica doesn't want to hear a word of what her sister is saying. The best response is for Marta and Evelyn to speak to Sandra Lagos once and for all. Mónica slams the fridge shut and clicks through TV channels with the remote control. The live transmission outside the front door of her house has resumed. For the time being, people continue to pray on automatic pilot. Inside, the doorbell won't stop ringing and the food is getting cold on the kitchen table.

Evelyn hears all of this from the part of the house that's off limits. She's thinking about things she'd rather not admit to. If her dad's alive, they'll go back to Ituzaingó and she won't matter to anybody, just like before. Everyone will want to talk to him. She's disappointed and doesn't like the good news. What she wants is for things to continue as they are.

Oh my god, she thinks, why does everyone care so much about finding a couple of mobile phones?

In the dark of the "study", Evelyn roots around for the small box with Miss Laura's mobile. She's spent all day thinking about burying it in the large flowerpot shaped like a swan—the one her aunt moved to the inner patio. She puts the mobile in the pocket of her sweatshirt and, resolved, walks down the hallway to the kitchen, intending to take advantage of the confusion. But Marta closes the door in her face, she doesn't even see her. And the last thing Evelyn hears is "calm down, Mónica, the man on the phone isn't Hugo, lower your voice and listen to me." Evelyn's plans collapse again. Damn it, goddamn it, she thinks, why isn't all this over already?

M ANCUSO AND OLGA manage to keep their heads above water until they hear El Rifle's news. Now things could go off in any direction. They're no longer in control of what happens, they know the current is going to carry them along. And neither of them is the sort to swim against it. Everything is going to speed up until it becomes a torrent, a waterfall. Olga has already recovered from the shock and glimpses the advantage of telling a half-truth. Mancuso has already vented his rage: via his thumbs, in a message to Domínguez to see what the fuck the detective has to say about Hugovíctor's mobile. Now, the two of them are rowing the same boat. What is there to be done? They're already rushing along midstream, aware that what comes next is falling into the void; there's no asking the water to run in the opposite direction. Mancuso and Olga are the sort that wait for the right moment to grab hold of the only branch, beating everyone else to it, or that jump onto shore as the boat falls vertically over the precipice and takes the more dim-witted among them with it. For the time being, each plays their part.

"I'm not saying Hugo's a saint, but he's not capable of getting away from a train wreck just like that, in front of all the police and firefighters. Domínguez seemed like a detective with a lot of experience. And you give me the impression of being very trustworthy."

"Fortunately, tomorrow we'll have the off-the-record DNA results. We hope your family will have some relief, Olga."

"What do you mean? That soon? What did you analyse? We didn't give you anything of Evelyn's."

"Her toothbrush, ma'am. Nowadays the lab can work wonders with a couple of cells. But just in case, you need to be prepared for the possibility that the remains are not your son-in-law."

"I don't think that'll happen. They must be Hugo. If not, the government, the police, everyone, will have made a fool of themselves. Wouldn't it be detrimental to you?"

"That's not the most important thing. Though I also want one of the bodies to be Hugovíctor and for this to end here."

"That's what I'm saying!"

"Which is why it would be good for you to start cooperating, Olga."

"**B**Y THE HOLY WOUNDS!"

Mónica's invocation means a number of things. Relief, now that she knows it's still possible that Hugo is dead and lost among pieces of the train. Rage, because her sister hid that his mobile ended up in Domínguez's hands. Anxiety, because they need to act, and it needs to be soon, and Marta still hasn't done anything.

"I'm not impulsive like you are, I have to think things over."

"Stop thinking, Marta! You've been thinking things over for two days while I've been organizing the prayers, the food, everything."

"Can't we stop for a minute and think?"

"What you need to think about is which father is best for Evelyn right now. Hugo is a victim. A vic-tim. The rest is unnecessary detail. React. We have to move on. And you have to be a protagonist."

Marta goes out to the inner patio for some air. From the kitchen, via the television, she hears the voices of Mónica's friends, who are keeping watch. The women are trying out official responses to the mysterious activation of Hugovíctor's mobile. She stops in front of the high wall that separates her from the outside. The shouts on the television don't reach her there. What does is a hum of prayers and lights. All Marta can see is the gleam from the television. She feels that on the other side of the wall, an immense wave is rising, and that it's going to swallow her. The image is from a movie that's always on cable and it's stayed with Marta. The movie isn't very good, but this part always pops into her head when she needs air. It's about a meteorite that's going to crash into Earth, fall into the ocean and cause a tsunami. The girl in the film decides not to flee. She remains on the beach, her hand in her father's, the two of them facing the sea. Marta likes this part, though it's very sad and makes her think that not even a love as great as theirs would have saved her from drowning. The girl and her father see it coming, the gigantic wave that's rising in front of them, that's going to swallow them forever, and they feel extreme anguish, but this is better than running, than trying to flee from the water that will trap them and drag them along just the same. A lot of people die fighting the current. Those who try to escape die anyway, those who climb the mountain die. Because the wave washes over everything and there's no way to avoid it. Marta sees herself holding Evelyn's hand, the two of them small in front of the wave that's so monstrous it's going to swallow them. Because that's what's going to happen. Because as soon as she goes through the front door, it's going to be like trying to control a tsunami that carries you away, bashes you into the rocks, doesn't even let you stick your head out to breathe, and then drags you onto the beach in pieces.

"It's not that big a deal, Marta," says Mónica's voice in the half-light of the patio. "It's like 'four crazy days', after this no one's going to remember you."

WHEN THEY ENTER the studio, Evelyn bolts. She lets go of Marta and bolts. Towards the lights. On the inside, she's entirely out of control. There's a stone in her throat and she's almost nauseous. Then air slowly begins to enter and she says a few clipped sentences into her grandmother's ear. Finally everything. Is turning out. All right. Olga worries the hug has gone on for too long, that it's awkward. She goes stiff as though she wants to pull away, and looks over the girl's shoulder at Sandra Lagos, so she'll intervene. Sandra Lagos takes a sip of water and checks with the director behind the camera. They have all the time in the world. Evelyn is crying. She's crying a lot. Olga sits her down, smooths the cornrows in her hair and takes her hand. She presses her lips together very tightly. My granddaughter Evelyn, she says. Marta is in the dark, waiting for them to tell her what to do.

Beto is also waiting to be told what to do. Olga finally called at night and told him to open the shop and stop fucking around on PlayStation. They'd think of something, she said. But for the time being, they have to return to daily life as best they can, and move on. Olga is admirable. She has so much conviction that Beto wonders if Tuesday morning actually happened. He would almost be convinced that Hugo's appearance was a dream, if the money, clothes and St Expeditus holy card hadn't disappeared.

Olga's right, they have to move on. Hugo was left behind. On the train or somewhere else—what difference does it make? Things won't be that bad if they continue as they have until now. The old lady is sorting it all out. Beto convinces himself of this too and turns up the volume on the shop's television. Word got out in the neighbourhood that he was a good friend of Hugovíctor's. Now everyone who passes by waves to him or pops in to give him a hug. But he hasn't made money all morning. And with everything that's going on, it'll be months before Olga gives him any dope to sell.

Beto's not an idiot. The blank look on his face—regardless

of what's going on—can be confusing. Olga calls him an idiot because it irritates her that he's so inaccessible. Beto is like the high wall of a dyke seen from below. You can't make out the other side, and have no idea what's going on there. Only the wall knows how much of an effort it goes to. A single, minimal fissure, and it collapses. Evelyn's tears, for example, are a crack in the wall. Evelyn is crying slowly, obediently, while Sandra Lagos asks her questions.

"My dad didn't do anything wrong," she says.

Sandra Lagos half smiles and half swallows the phlegm in her throat before responding. "Of course he didn't," she says, and opens her arms, "there's no questioning that, there isn't. What could be wrong with taking the train to work?"

Beto can't bear this because he's not an idiot. Because it's one thing for a friend to put his mess in a bag and take it far away, and another for Evelyn to have to go on television and cry softly to clean up her father's filth.

He stands there for a while, gripping the counter, kicking at the wall, willing Evelyn to stop crying. Olga's always telling him he has nothing and it's true, but of everything he doesn't have, what he cares most about is Evelyn. He imagines losing her would be like losing Pamela. At first, he couldn't bear it, but time passed and he got used to it. Then he was ready for anything. After what happened with the motorcycle, nothing has been able to hurt him or drive him mad. He does what he has to do and moves on. Because what's done is done. It's this sort of determination that's building in him again as he watches Evelyn cry on television.

When she has stopped crying, Marta appears and speaks with a certainty and strength that Beto has never seen. He figures it's because she's convinced that Hugo is gone. It's the first time in ten years she's looked straight ahead to say something. Marta always averts her gaze towards the floor or a window when she's talking to someone. She's a wall just like he is. You never know what's behind her. And for Beto, this is like a magnet. Whenever he visits Hugo he tries to spend some time with her, the two of them talking about any old thing and not looking at each other. He hasn't seen her since the night he showed up with an excuse to take the bag and she didn't notice a thing. But Marta has known about everything for a while. That's what Beto understands now, when she looks Sandra Lagos in the eye to speak. Olga always tells him he should redo his life, now that he's earning money. Marta filters through him like a fissure in the wall. This is the sort of thing that's going through his mind when people think nothing is.

His determination and the coffee wake him up. A strong desire to move takes hold of him, but he doesn't know in which direction. The waitress from the café has returned for his empty cup and the small plate that had toast on it. She wipes the crumbs off with her hand and now that he's looking a bit better than he did earlier, she says, "It's so sad about your friend, you must be having a tough go of it." And he looks at her the way she's looking at him, pulls her to him, his hands on her arse, and sticks his tongue in her mouth. Because when Beto emerges from a state of lethargy, he turns into a bundle of directionless impulses with no clear instructions. He's ready. Enough PlayStation.

M ARTA IS TALKING a lot on television. She knows she's talking, is fully aware of it, and yet she can't contain herself. As soon as the words leave her mouth, they get away from her. It seems to be going well because everyone is looking at her attentively and nodding. It's as if Sandra Lagos were holding her hand. She makes it easy for Marta. She says a few things and all Marta has to do is finish her sentence. And while Marta is doing all this, she's thinking about one thing: what she's planned to say about the mobile. It's not that difficult. The family knows nothing and are asking themselves the same question everyone is. The most important thing is not to make a mistake about the mobile. And that occupies all of her thoughts. The rest is just talking and responding to Sandra Lagos, and though everything seems to be going well, Marta remains alert, because at any moment they could ask her about Hugovíctor's mobile.

"I just called him Hugo." Marta hears herself say these words, the only ones she hasn't planned, and for the first time, she feels certain she won't see him again.

A comfortable sadness is beginning to occupy the space taken by anxiety, and because Marta has been thinking so much, she doesn't realize that it's all over. That she's already walking down a hallway, the lights have been turned off, and that she wasn't asked about Hugovíctor's mobile. That they're giving Evelyn a Coke and fixing her braids, and that Olga is pushing her towards a small room with a sofa and mirror surrounded by white lights, where they'll be left alone. That Olga is entering behind her and slamming the door.

"Do you mind telling me what's gotten into you? You didn't call this whole time."

A NOTHER DAY and Hugo hasn't showered. Spot has been following him, but from a distance. After his second bottle last night, he may have taken things out on the dogs. He can't remember. And now it's all going wrong at the parrilla. The only thing he asks of them is to change the channel, to put something else on. Who could eat with that girl crying on Sandra Lagos's programme? There are more than six hundred channels, there's no need to eat lunch like this.

He asks the waiter nicely. He's been a client for three days, eating and paying. When the waiter returns with his chorizo, Hugo lets the bloke know he saw him come and go without bothering to change the channel. The waiter says the other diners want to watch it. The man at the table next to him, the same man who was there last night, explains that the girl is the daughter of Hugovíctor, the one from the train. Why do they want to see her? Hugo thinks, angered. He stands up suddenly, stumbles, goes to the bathroom, returns with his face wet and makes his way to the television. Only he can't reach the buttons, the set is mounted too high up. He jumps a few times to get at the plug, but he loses his balance and his patience, and so he climbs onto the counter where, on his belly, he looks for the remote control the sons of bitches at the parrilla have hidden.

They pull him down. Three of them take him out to the pavement and give him a shove. Hugo ends up in the middle of the street. He turns around and is at the parrilla's door again, right as they close it in his face. Evelyn isn't on TV any more but he kicks at the glass just the same. "Tell her that her father isn't coming back and stop bothering her," he says, defiant.

"Why don't you go drop dead?" yells a large bloke, who throws him to the ground and pins him by the neck, as though he's going to punch him in the nose and break it. The bloke doesn't even recognize Hugo from up close, because the more they hate him the less likely they are to realize he's Hugovíctor. In the end, they spare his face and tell him not to return. The waiter comes out and launches Hugo's backpack after him. He's lucky the bottle of whisky doesn't break. Spot is barking but it's not clear at whom.

Hugo sits down in the basilica for a while to think. He drinks whisky with holy water from the plastic container. Greyhound isn't there. He remembers a movie with a bloke who went to a casino to drink and fuck around until he'd blown all his cash. Until he'd died. What was it called? It was in Las Vegas. He thinks this is a good idea. He could do the same thing, only in Luján and on the Rollercoaster. Make himself disappear. It's what's best for Evelyn. In the movie, there was a beautiful woman. But it would all be a big shit-show if he did it in Luján. Spot isn't outside any more either.

For a while, Hugo looks for the dog and he goes as far as the river without finding him. The place is practically deserted. The pirate ship ride moves from one side to the other on its own, with no kid in it. A gypsy is smoking under the sun. Hugo asks her for a cigarette and shows her the palm of his hand. The ghost ship wobbles, the rusted iron screeching. The gypsy looks Hugo in the eye and says "get lost".

Hugo loses himself in the afternoon. He wanders for a while along the trail that borders the river. After the first bridge, it becomes a path of broken paving stones invaded by weeds and surrounded by thickets. The shoreline is a swamp that's wider than the actual riverbed. Past the second bridge, the water no longer flows. It's still like everything else. Only the plastic supermarket bags move a little, tangled up in the branches. Hugo keeps walking until he goes round a bend and can no longer see the basilica, the amusement park rides, the smoke, the kids getting out of school. It's a landscape that's become familiar to him in a short time. He reaches the part where the river turns black and narrow and the trees form a gallery around it. It's like entering a tunnel. He walks another 300 metres through it, climbing over enormous roots and sinking into the mud.

He leaves his sneakers next to the trunk of a willow tree. Then he tosses his backpack onto the ground and empties what remains of the whisky. Hesitates. He takes the money he has left out of the backpack and drops a lit match onto it, setting the pack on fire. While he puts the bills into his trousers, he walks out into the water.

OLGA HAS TOUGH things to say and she does so without raising her voice. Marta has been preparing for this moment the whole taxi ride from Colón. Her whole life. But now the same thing is happening as always. She's paralysed like an animal under threat. Olga belongs to one of those rare species that eats their young. One by one, Marta went over the words she was going to say to her mother. But she's not able to say them because Olga starts talking and she doesn't stop—something she's good at. She doesn't grant Marta a moment of silence, a breath, doesn't have the decency to let her speak. Olga has found a piece of paper towel somewhere and is folding it in two, four, eight, pressing a Pearly Pink nail into the creases. Each of them marks a point in her argument.

"You know how much tuition is at Los Santos Ángeles Custodios."

Evelyn wants to stop crying because her eyeliner is going to run. While her mum and grandma talk, she's taken to see the dressing rooms. She hopes they stay in Buenos Aires one more day so she can go to Martín's birthday party with her cornrows and super HD make-up. The girls who work at the channel promised they'd do her hair and make-up again for the leavers' prom. They're all awesome. But they've never heard of her school, Los Santos Ángeles Custodios. "It must be in the suburbs," they say to each other. Evelyn hears them and feels ugly and stupid, and she doesn't know why.

Olga is on the second fold of her paper towel and has moved on to the subject of Hugo.

"About that Cristaldo kid, things like that happen all the time in this business. That's why I didn't want to mix business with family. Beto was the one who got Hugo involved. And you never asked where the money was coming from."

"I didn't know the name."

"Of what?"

"Of the kid."

"He was a delinquent, Marta. He got involved in my... I'd had it all sorted out with his uncle. Let it go, it doesn't matter. The problem is that Hugo handled it very poorly."

Olga folds the paper in eight. "What did you expect? For me to tell you everything?"

Marta is unable to say anything. She dissolves to the point of just nodding.

Evelyn has fallen asleep on a prop armchair in Sandra Lagos's studio. Someone walks by and covers her with the leavers' sweatshirt from Los Santos Ángeles Custodios. The technicians turn off and unplug everything. Olga taps her Pearly Pink nails on the counter in the dressing room, her eyes fixed on Marta, who looks down at her own hands. Someone knocks on the door and lets them know the taxis have arrived. One is going to Ituzaingó and the other to Retiro Station.

"Go live in Colón for a while. Settle in with your sister, say hello for me. It's what's best for everyone."

That's what Marta had been thinking of saying and doing, but Olga beat her to it. She'd also wanted to say, I'm lost, Mum, dried up, I want to look at a river until my fear of drowning goes away. But it was her mother who said things. And that's not the same.

THE SELFIE EVELYN TAKES with the buses behind her is dark and sad, even with her make-up and hair done. Fame is the biggest disappointment of her life. She tries out different filters on her tablet to improve the photo. That way she can put it on Instagram when she has Wi-Fi. Her mum points to a seat and buys her a hot dog while she talks to a police officer. It's Domínguez, Evelyn is sure of it. He's not wearing a uniform, but she hasn't forgotten his face. And this is after barely seeing it from the side the night he went to their house to take her away. It's a good thing Miss Laura's mobile is still well hidden in Colón.

A few metres away from Evelyn, Domínguez and Marta are also eating hot dogs. They'd agreed to meet to tie up loose ends, and they understand each other immediately.

"I wanted to see if it would get me somewhere." The detective has no better answer to explain why he kept Hugo's mobile after finding it on the platform.

"It was something like that for me too," Marta says honestly when the detective asks her why she fled that night.

"Like what?"

"Like what you said, to see if I could get somewhere."

They promise to call each other if they have news of Hugo, but Marta is more concerned with other things.

"I ask you not to tell Sandra Lagos anything. Or El Rifle Barrios."

"I don't know those people. Who are they?"

HUGO IS WAITING. His body is barely moving. The thick black water is up to his nose. He's in the middle of the river, as deep as he could go. His feet sink into the mud, but the water still doesn't cover him. It should at least be entering through his pores. He makes a mental list of the things that will get into his blood. Shit, venom, rubbish, rats, dead vermin, puppies, lost children, diesel oil, kerosene, ugly fish, burnt cooking oil, bones, cadavers no one is looking for and a thick liquid that looks like milk as it drains from a pipe a few metres away, where it enters the river and merges with the black water like a lethal injection.

Time passes and the river is still. It's so dead the air doesn't even smell like rot. There are just traces of the burnt plastic that was his backpack and the distant scent of recently cut grass. The sun goes down behind the trees and Hugo starts to feel cold, then nauseous. He vomits and ingests the black water; it enters his mouth, his nose, filling his lungs, loosening his sphincter. He lifts his feet out of the mud, draws his legs in to bear the pain in his writhing gut. He takes advantage of the situation and lets his head sink, stretching his body out belly down, his arms in a cross. The vomit floats around him and mixes with everything else.

Hugo struggles to remain below the surface but the black water pushes him up, forces him to breathe. When he opens his eyes, he's in the same place. The trees are still, a darker and darker shade of green. What kind of river is this? he thinks. It doesn't even have a current, enough force to push him towards a larger arm, one that will devour and sink him in violent brown water, turning him into nothing, carrying him to another river that's wider and blue and that will finally toss him into the sea and oblivion.

It doesn't move, the piece-of-shit river he's in.

TALKING TO MANCUSO is like the opposite of an interrogation: all the softening up isn't so that Domínguez reveals something, but so he gets the message crystal clear, well wrapped in wine and words and digressions about how a chorizo steak should be cooked, along with a supposed interest in the Cristaldo case. The dinner began early but it's already getting late. Domínguez went straight from the bus terminal at Retiro Station to the parrilla in the centre of Haedo. He's not saying anything. He's waiting. At some point, the department head will make his intentions clear. There's never a literal message, exact words that can be quoted, an explicit order. A dinner invitation from Mancuso is never a good thing. They've now moved on to coffee.

"What invention in the last fifty... what am I saying, not fifty, let's say thirty years, fucked with everything?"

The time has come for Domínguez to be Mancuso's doormat, the wall on the pelota court that returns the ball precisely where the department head wants it. Domínguez draws the game out.

"The internet? GPS? Kiwis?"

"DNA, you idiot."

"I see we're getting into this now."

Domínguez feels his arse tighten and his back straighten, announcing he's on duty. He moves three squares back.

"Get into what, you arsehole? There's no talking to you, you're suspicious of everything. Have a whisky. Take it easy. You're a workaholic, do you know what that is? When you retire you won't know what to do with yourself. You need to start enjoying life a little, man. You're gonna get depressed."

"DNA isn't an invention, it's a discovery."

Mancuso aims at Domínguez with his index finger, his thumb pointed upwards, like he's holding a pistol.

"Well done on the vocabulary. That's why I like to read your reports. You're cultured."

Mancuso begins to swirl the ice around in his glass. He fixes his gaze on the TV until Domínguez gets irritated. The department head always chooses a table that leaves his interlocutor without a means of escape. When what's on the screen distracts Mancuso, like it does right now—El Rifle Barrios is talking to a kid in a neck brace with his torso bandaged—the conversation lightens up.

"What's the problem with DNA tests? They save lives…" Domínguez says, going at Mancuso a little, to move the conversation along.

"For every bloke you save from a disease, for every vaccine you invent, every… How often? Every twenty years?… For every one of these isolated events, fifty thousand lives are destroyed. Think about it. What if all the married broads you fucked go and get their kids' DNA tested? One of them is going to be yours. You're screwed, the father's screwed, the kid's screwed, the broad's screwed. There's thousands of cases like that. In the past, a woman went to the hospital to have her baby, and say they gave her the wrong kid, what was the problem? There wasn't one. The other family brought a child home too, am I right?"

"Well, but you'd be living a lie…"

"What lie? That's in two or three cases, a kid snatched, things like that. I won't deny it happens. But I'm talking about the majority of cases. The majority were screwed when they got the result. You can't live in peace any more."

Domínguez gives in and brings up the subject once and for all.

"It's allowed us to find suspects with the certainty that…"

"We've always found suspects."

"But with the laboratory, you can be more certain you haven't accused someone who's innocent."

"Innocent of what? Think about it. Maybe you placed some bloke at a scene that wasn't his, but that doesn't make him innocent. He'd have gone to the slammer for one case instead of another, that's all. They're always guilty of something, in the end everything balances out. You're talking like a lawyer. That's something you could do when you retire, study law."

"So do we have the results for the remains from the train?"

Mancuso watches the television for a few seconds and then responds.

"None of the parts are him. It was all for shit. We still have the problem of finding Hugovíctor. Though you've got the case solved."

"I don't have it solved because…"

"The prints are enough, stop fucking around. You're digressing. The most logical conclusion is that the remains are Hugovíctor. Deal's good for everyone. What's the point of having the DNA of a couple of bums no one's claiming if we can't check it against anything? Understand my reasoning here. It's not that I'm against science, progress; what I'm saying is that in a case like this, the laboratory just complicates matters. Right now the shitshow is more political than anything else. People are losing it and for good reason. They can't even find a poor bloke who died in an accident. But you know who's going to take the blame when he finally turns up?"

"Well, maybe he left…"

"How could he have left? Say he survived, the first thing he would have done is get in touch with his family, am I right?"

"That depends. If you're wanted for homicide…"

"The bloke didn't know he was wanted. He'd already left for work when you showed up at his house, am I right?"

Domínguez has taken the bait. He shouldn't have said so much. There's no point in arguing with Mancuso.

"Look. There's a single weak spot and you know what it is: Hugovíctor's mobile. If you're sure the bloke's alive and that he fled, I can get them to track the device. I'm surprised you haven't requested this be done. You're under stress, you're forgetting simple shit. Do you want me to have his phone tracked? If you want this shitshow to fall on our shoulders instead of the government's, and to turn us into the idiots who let him go, I'll request one and that'll be that, we'll see what happens. Wherever we find the mobile, chances are good he's there—wouldn't you say?"

"No, because maybe the phone is among the pieces of metal…"

"Which is where sooner or later they're going to find poor Hugovíctor! Don't overthink this."

Mancuso puts his second glass of whisky down as though he intends to shatter it and fixes his gaze on the TV again. This is him showing Domínguez he's done. But something happens. The detective notices a fleeting movement in his boss's jaw and turns to see what caused it. The bandaged kid is still there, talking to a journalist who looks familiar to Domínguez because he also hosts the football programme that's always on at the pizzeria. "This survivor saw Hugovíctor at the Posadas Hospital," it says on the screen. Two waiters plant themselves in front of the TV and raise the volume. Mancuso returns to the conversation as if this was of no importance.

"A government-directed operetta. At this point, they don't know what to make up. Look at this lout and tell me people are going to believe him more than they do a lady like Olga."

"What does that have to do with this?"

The department head leans back and opens his arms, showing the palms of his hands.

"If you're convinced, keep looking, keep digging. I have a good deal of respect for your work. I know zilch about homicides. What I want to do is protect my people. And if you oppose poor Olga and her son-in-law, Hugovíctor, you'll do us all in. I don't understand you. You want to prove you let a bloke escape, you want everyone to find out, when it's clear we're dealing with another problem here. I'm telling you this for your sake, okay? I have to deal with this shitshow regardless, because the force that can't find him among the pieces of metal are my people too. But, hey, if now it turns out that the poor victim of this mess is an assassin on the run…"

"If he ended up on the train, he's a victim regardless."

"What country do you live in, Domínguez?"

Mancuso asks for the bill. "Look how much you ate, you're expensive, man."

He makes the same sarcastic remark he always does, but Domínguez knows he's exaggerating his lack of concern, that he doesn't want to sign the bill and put his black card away until he's done watching the interview with the survivor. The kid's told the same story several times but the journalist wants more details.

"So you asked him for his name and what did he say?"

"He told me it was St Expeditus."

El Rifle Barrios is a little disconcerted by the kid's answer. "Oh, so then you're not sure it was Hugovíctor?"

Domínguez's own car is parked at the parrilla's entrance, but he has to accept the department head's offer for a ride.

This is not Mancuso being kind. Instead, the drive is going to be the last act, when all the lines of argument fall into place and Mancuso comes out of this unscathed. It's as if he's got a cadaver in the boot—he's set the air conditioner to the temperature of a meat locker. To sober him up after the wine and whisky.

"I'm not saying you shouldn't look for him. You do your job the way you like to: on your own, with a low profile. Let me take charge of the whole spectacle. You do your work quietly. That is unless you want Sandrita Lagos to drive you mad for dirtying the image of a poor worker from Ituzaingó?"

"Who's Sandrita Lagos?"

"She has that programme on Channel 5."

"Oh. I don't watch television."

"What a character you are. I'm not saying you shouldn't solve the case, what I'm asking for is a bit of timing," Mancuso continues, the last word in English. "Sooner or later, this lad Madrid will turn up on the train, Olga will no longer be news, the government will be left with the shitshow, and then bam, that's when you pull out the file: crime solved, no one bothers you, your record is still better than Barça's. Do you see what I'm saying? You still count the case as solved. And don't tell me that in your old age all of a sudden you play by the rules because as far as procedure and paperwork go, you've always been decidedly weak. Though I wouldn't say you're like the characters on that series... What's it called? The one on HBO, with that bloke and the broad. She's a good actress, a bit too skinny, no arse, tits, nothing, but it's a good series. Have you seen it?"

"I don't know, Mancuso, I told you I don't have cable."

"But you can download it, man, it's really good. You have to make some changes in your life. When you retire I'm going to take away your weapon so you don't do yourself in. I can get a Smart TV for you tomorrow."

"Hold on, wait a second, what for? I don't want a television."

"It's not a television, it's a Smart TV; it's a whole other thing, you'll see, you won't regret it. I'll get one for you, you won't have to pay a peso. All right, get out, it's late. I'll send it to you tomorrow. Relax a little, I'm not going to kill anyone to get you a Smart TV. Watch that series, I'm telling you you'll like it. They all do their jobs the way you like things done: by the rules, not a single mistake."

T HE SUN'S RAYS bounce off Jesus and his tarp, intensifying the light and heat. Mónica's friends have been praying for two days, and their skin is burning, their eyes are tired, and their hair is a mess. Yesterday's make-up has diluted on Evelyn's face, and thick brown drops are falling down her cheeks. They look like the Christ on the grille's blood. She fans herself with a magazine that has her picture on the cover. All she wants to do is go inside and lie down on the cool floor of her aunt's house, but she had wanted to be outside so badly that now she can't leave. In the only bit of shade on the pavement, Marta and Mónica are talking to Sandra Lagos's producer quietly.

Some of the people still there praying are about to leave, because during the hotter months, the weekend begins on Fridays at noon when the kids get off school, and everyone heads to the river with baskets full of sandwiches. Evelyn watches a small group of secondary-school students as they walk past, carrying two-litre bottles of soda. She loses focus beyond the part of the street that rises, where the breeze comes off the water. The burning hot tarp warms her back. The only cameraman who's working tells her they're done and gives her a plastic cup of grapefruit soda. But Evelyn stays put, next to Jesus's heart, waiting for something amazing to happen.

There's a schism in the air in Mónica's quarters. On the opposite pavement, a dissident group is muttering something about the boy who says he saw Hugovíctor alive, but mostly they're talking about Marta, who's not crying, not praying, not holding out hope, not doing anything to give them the confidence they need to keep up the cause. Many have left because they've lost faith. Those who remain aren't praying, but have pounced on a box of empanadas they bought by taking up a collection. As of today, the casino is no longer sending food.

OLGA DOESN'T LIKE to eat empanadas out of the box. She heats them up a little in the oven and sets them on a small plate. Beto brought over a half-dozen because he didn't know Mancuso had also been invited. He didn't even know who Mancuso was. He found out as he was entering Olga's house and she was closing the door. The department head asked Beto to take a seat in front of him. Beto deserves credit for the composure and serenity with which he received the shock. It's not cold blood. Cold blood is emptiness, the absence of emotions. Composure is the ability to bury them. Olga considers it an important trait. She herself has cultivated it. To do all that needed to be done until she was widowed, to take care of her daughters and distance herself from them now that they're a hindrance, to be left alone. The Morón Department Head doesn't cause Olga to bat an eye. They're in the same boat and will row in the direction that's necessary to keep themselves afloat.

Beto is concerned. About the chicken empanadas. He hopes there will be enough, and apologizes: a couple of empanadas per person is really just a starter.

"An appetizer," Mancuso interjects in English, and it's the

first thing he says, because he didn't even open his mouth to say hello to Beto.

The two of them eat with gusto. Olga doesn't take a bite. She's got her eye on Beto, who looks calm, though you never know how he's going to react. People say he's been this way since the motorcycle accident. It's like he's forever stuck on the shoulder, tottering, watching the rest of the world pass him by at full speed. That's how he ended up—it's as though he were still stunned. And at the same time willing to take a step forwards and have it all be over. He's dangerous but also the ideal candidate when it comes to resolving matters. When all that's left on the plate are Olga's two empanadas, Mancuso begins with his digressions.

"It's called an appetizer because it whets the appetite. You eat a couple of empanadas and you end up hungrier than you were before."

He sips his wine, which has ice in it, and waits for the other two to show their cards. Olga folds a paper towel on the table. Beto can't handle the silence.

"Has there been any news of Hugo?"

"No need to pretend, Beto, Mr Mancuso is up to speed."

After doing her part, Olga bites into an empanada. That is, if the pieces of rubbish filled with air that the wretched Beto brought can be called empanadas.

A T DON GUIDO's the chicken filling is juicy. And there's plenty of it. Rather than leftover bits, the empanadas seem to be made of very generous chunks of chicken breast. Ramírez chews while he holds Domínguez's gaze, which is like a mule's. He doesn't help him, and lets him run out of praise for the empanadas, at which point he'll have no choice but to return to the case of that kid, Carlos David, and the whole Hugovíctor mess. Ramírez knew of the Cristaldos in the west end of the city, but he'd heard nothing about that lady, Olga.

"Well, what do you want to know? If Mancuso hadn't wanted to avoid going at it with Cristaldo's uncle, this homicide wouldn't have gotten any attention or a budget. And now it's a file no one wants on their desk. As if it's homicide's fault that trains crash."

Domínguez is talking as if he weren't disgruntled. He avoids looking at Ramírez, takes the remote control off the counter at Don Guido's and flips through channels on the TV. He leaves it on Channel 5, which is transmitting from the front of Mónica's house, where the now-reduced group of neighbourhood women are still praying and passing around the *mate*. This image takes up a small window on the bottom right of the screen. Evelyn's braids have come undone and she looks like she can handle no more. Off to the side, Marta and a young woman are serving themselves grapefruit soda. The woman is holding a microphone so it's ready to use when she gets the order. A lad from another channel walks by, rolling up a cable on his arm. When this last on-air broadcast from Colón is over, they'll all say goodbye and wish each other good luck, just like any other group of people who have spent time together on a course or travelling on a tour. The full screen shows the studio of someone named Sandra Lagos. In it, people Domínguez doesn't know argue over whose head is going to roll.

The detective is still clicking through the channels, though there's no news about the DNA on any of them. Maybe Mancuso held on to the information, Ramírez speculates. Domínguez is convinced that it's already been circulated, which is what happens whenever they get results back from the laboratory, but that nobody knows what to do with it.

"This uncertainty isn't good for anyone. It's a shitshow."

"**I**F HUGO'S BODY is found among the pieces of metal tonight, the shitshow ends here. At least for those of us who didn't fuck things up: you, me, Olga."

Mancuso pushes a bundle wrapped in a jacket across the table. Beto gets a sense of its weight before putting it in his backpack. As though Olga were waiting for them to say her name, she enters the scene, returning from the kitchen with their coffees.

"I've already explained to Mr Mancuso that you had nothing to do with that other matter, that you just wanted to help Hugo out."

"You didn't leave any prints, you're careful." Mancuso pulls his chair over to Beto's and gives him one of his looks from below. "That's why I trust you. Trust me that everything you need will be there. You won't have to carry a thing. You'll return as light as you left."

Beto puts the jacket on and Mancuso explains which route will get him around the tolls. There's a heavy silence, then further instructions.

"Take cash for petrol. Don't even think of using your card. And don't do anything else. Carrying the bag alone on the motorcycle was madness. You're mad, no one does that for a friend. I'm not asking that much of you."

His helmet already on, Beto shakes his head. Mancuso understands Beto to be saying he's right, but instead it's: How dare you compare yourself to Hugo, and what the fuck were you talking about when you said I was going to return light? But there's no point in losing his shit now. He can't put the business off much longer. As he's leaving, Beto hears the department head tell the old lady to take a seat. He deals with her too.

"We're going to put your business in a bit of order, Olga, before it occurs to someone to take a closer look."

"UNTIL HUGO SHOWS UP, everyone's going to be taking a closer look at things to see what they can find. Imagine if what they find is Cristaldo. They're all going to look like fools. All of them."

Domínguez reinforces "all of them" by raising his right index finger and drawing a circle in the air that includes the television, the pizzeria, the government, the department, everyone minus him and Ramírez. The case, the actual case, that is, who killed who, has been solved. For the homicide department there's not much more to do. He raises his shoulders and the palms of his hands towards Ramírez, who allows himself to be persuaded. Facts are facts. There's the body with more prints on it than a public toilet. And there are Cristaldo's two neighbours, who saw Hugo arrive and the fight. This Hugo chap isn't exactly a professional. He wasn't.

"The facts," says Domínguez.

He lifts the only empanada left a few centimetres off the plate and then puts it back down—it's his way of emphasizing that Cristaldo's cadaver is a fact. A fact represented, on the table at Don Guido's, by the chicken empanada, just as the glass of beer he sets down brusquely next to the plate becomes Hugovíctor, who all evidence is pointing to. The bottle is the third fact that Domínguez positions next to the empanada and the glass: Hugovíctor has not appeared. But this is a matter that exceeds the homicide department, and to illustrate this, Domínguez slides the bottle to the other end of the table. It's all crystal clear.

Domínguez takes a sip of the warm beer in the murderer-glass and asks Ramírez if he'd like another bottle in an attempt at changing the subject. He has no reason to give Ramírez explanations. What people need to understand is that the facts are one thing and how they're communicated is another. Headquarters is responsible for communication. Hugo Víctor Lamadrid will not cease to be who he is next week or the week after when he appears—that is, if he appears—and things fall into place. The crime has been solved and the pieces fit together, which is the work of detectives like Domínguez and Ramírez. What Mancuso does, whether he wants to release one piece of information first and another later, is not homicide's problem. It's a communication issue. Another bottle of beer arrives and Domínguez serves them both. He wonders why he ordered another drink when he has nothing left to say.

"Did you know that Mancuso has a degree?" Domínguez asks, pointing at Ramírez with the remote control. But even this doesn't get a word out of him. Ramírez shakes his head.

"In marketing." Domínguez says this with a half-smile and a sarcastic tone, wanting to start a conversation about how little respect the marketing department deserves. Ramírez does respond this time, but it's to talk about another matter.

"So what do we do about the mobile?"

"What mobile?"

"The one you kept."

Domínguez laughs. It's been a while since he had a partner. He likes this Ramírez fellow quite a bit. He goes out to the pavement for a smoke.

M ARTA STUBS her cigarette out in the ashtray on the night table. Mónica wrinkles her nose and waves her hand to get rid of the smoke. She's trying to fall asleep, a cold gel mask over her eyes.

"When things go back to normal and we can use the other rooms, I don't want you smoking in here."

Evelyn is exploring her belly button with a magnifying glass. Seated on the floor, folded over herself, she digs around in the labyrinth, unable to reach the end, while out of the corner of her eye she watches a video on her aunt's mobile.

Ten things your belly button says about you. Round: you're an optimistic person. Closed up tight: you're mysterious, somewhat enigmatic. A spiral: you'll experience some difficulty in your relationships with the opposite sex; you should choose a man with a good belly button.

She can't decide what shape her belly button is and what this means for her future.

"Aunt Mónica, the man who said he saw dad at the hospital, is he doing it for the money?"

"What money, Evelyn, if there's no reward?"

Mónica is in a foul mood. The Hugo situation is dragging on and getting complicated. Two days ago she was being offered whatever she needed. The whole city, the people she knows, wanted to be seen next to her, praying, at the door to her house. The casino sent the boys over in corporate attire. But they've had enough and want to know when she's coming back. Or worse, they're distrustful. All of this could ruin her image, her reputation, the only thing she has. Years of personal marketing. Mónica is trustworthy. Reliable. That's why women turn to her when they need to improve their sex lives. It's why the casino is going to give her a senior position working the roulette wheels. And now Hugo is destroying her credibility. The body of Hugo that won't turn up.

"Two days of praying for nothing."

I N LUJÁN, metallic music is coming from the loudspeakers, the ride machinery is making noise, the smell of burnt sugar is in the air, and things are bustling. It's a Friday. No one looks Hugo in the face. He takes a bite out of a caramel apple and lines up to ride the Super 8 again. There are a lot of people around. The couple behind him keeps a distance of at least two metres. The boys in front of him move off to the side of the queue. Because he smells of whisky and rancid water.

With the money Mancuso gave him, Beto buys a key chain with the virgin and the Chevrolet logo on it. He drives slowly along a road parallel to the coast, leaves the motorcycle under the second bridge, and then takes a good look at the river from above. Towards the back, it flows around several bends and the trees form a gallery. Like a cave. He returns to the amusement park area on foot. He doesn't expect to find Hugo on the rollercoaster called Rollercoaster, but he looks for him there anyway, walks around a few times, and then takes the chairlift across the river.

Beto rides alone, even though there are two seats. A couple of blokes sit down behind him—the men Mancuso sent. The chairlift climbs slowly. To the right, the basilica's towers rise even higher. Below, people are screaming on a machine that sways from side to side until they're upside down as it rotates on its axis. Beto doesn't get why people ride it. When he crosses the river, he reaches for the bundle in his backpack, takes out the gun and puts it in the inside pocket of his jacket.

He gets off the chairlift and goes straight to the Super 8. He makes Hugo out from a distance because of the space between him and the people around him, and because Hugo is wearing his clothes, which look like they've been washed in petrol. Hugo doesn't see Beto coming: he's concentrating, his head back, his eyes following the trajectory of the little car sliding along the metallic structure—something he's always done—hypnotized by the movement, attracted by the cycle that's the same each time. A dog with a spot on it is looking up, just like Hugo. Two other dogs run back and forth, between the ends of the wire fence, crazed, looking for a gap where they can get into the ride area.

Hugo notices Beto when he's very close. He stumbles a little when he sees his friend, but it might be the alcohol. Beto can't read his eyes, because his baseball cap is pulled down low. Spot goes up to Beto, smells him, growls and leaves. Hugo smiles with his filthy teeth.

"Can you believe the Super 8's here?" he says and points to the basilica. "Next to God."

He gives Beto a token and they get into the car together. The ride starts with the sound of an old train on worn tracks. Tra-trac tra-trac tra-trac. Two curves to the right and a sudden climb. Tra-trac tra-trac. Their arms wrapped around the security bar, facing forward. Tra-trac. Tra-trac. They reach the highest point and are suspended there for a second. Tra-trac.

"How did you find me?"

"You used my transit pass, idiot."

The car drops, Hugo raises his arms and lets out a scream. Beto doesn't. Then they go around turns that Hugo knows by heart. Four to the right, each slower and lower down, his body tilted forwards, falling onto Beto. When they get out of the car, Rottweiler nips at their feet. There's no need for them to agree on what to do next. There will be no second ride. They walk while Hugo talks excitedly and Beto listens in silence, which is what they always did after a ride at Italpark.

"Know what? These past few days, I understood. I understood it all. The momentum comes from the first fall. It's the only one that matters. Everything that comes after it is downhill, even when it seems you're going up. If you go up a little, it's so you fall with more force. You're falling from the start. Like in life itself, Beto." Hugo makes a dramatic gesture, like a bow, a salute at the end of the play.

And then Beto checks the bundle in his jacket, lowers his eyes and says they're going to have to go over to the river.

S EATED ON THE SHORE, Evelyn keeps watch. She doesn't take her eyes off the water. After their siesta, her mum and aunt decided to get used to her dad not being there and to leave the house. No one is looking at them on the beach. Either that, or they're pretending not to know who they are. Evelyn is waiting for a whirlpool. Sooner or later, one will pass by. They're not easy to see. The calm surface gives hardly any indication of the turbulent water below. You can't trust what looks still and gentle and always stays the same. You could be floating calmly and all of a sudden a force could come along, drag you under and carry you away. Even if you knew how to swim. Because the whirlpool would be stronger than you.

A whole family was fishing in a lake in Córdoba and a whirlpool carried them away. It was like someone had pulled out a plug, suddenly the water swallowed them all up. There were people on the shore and they didn't see anything. Not even the boat was left floating. Whirlpools are as small as a belly button on the surface, but deep under water they never end, you can't see the end. The baby survived. It showed up on a beach in South Africa where it lives with its new family. But no one knows what the whirlpool was like on the inside, because the baby doesn't remember any of it.

There was just one man who survived to tell what it was like. He was fishing with his brothers and a gigantic whirlpool dragged him to the depths of the abyss. The others died but he made it out by clinging to a wooden barrel. He was saved because the barrel was a cylinder and wood floats. People sometimes make the mistake of thinking they'll be saved by grabbing hold of something big and strong. But not that man. He let go and allowed himself to be carried along. Her aunt's always saying the same thing—that you have to let go and allow yourself to be carried along. But the fisherman's story is a lot older. And it's true, because Evelyn read about it at school. In the end, he turned up alive on the shore. He'd been in the whirlpool for only an hour. But in that time, he'd aged ten years. His hair was white and he had a lot of wrinkles. No one recognized him and they thought he was crazy. Whirlpools are scary and that's why nobody wants to talk about them. People point to the river and say look how calm the water is today. Until one day a whirlpool comes along and it takes you away.

Evelyn thinks about this bottomless spiral of silent fury and feels like she might be sick, like when her aunt took her to the casino for the first time. She'd stared at the roulette wheel for so long she almost fainted. But in spite of the fact that she gets dizzy thinking about it, Evelyn has made up her mind: she intends to spend the whole summer if necessary, waiting for the whirlpool that will swallow up what needs to be left behind. She waits with the water brushing against the soles of her feet, her eyes on the deepest part of the river, where her opportunity will come from, while her mum and aunt talk and argue some more and drink *mate* under a tree. Evelyn feels that conversations and days are like belly buttons that go round in circles and get twisted up and have ends that you never see.

Then, at a distance that seems neither far nor close, a branch floats by, motionless, before it suddenly sinks, just like that, and in the still water, everything remains the same. A few small boys fight over who gets to climb onto a tyre that's been turned into a giant floater and a man pulls them with a rope. Evelyn figures the fierce current lurking in the depths won't carry them away. She goes in slowly until the water reaches her knees and tries to fix her gaze on the whirlpool again, to trap it and to guess where it's coming from and where it's going. She hears Mónica's voice behind her, a little above the hum of the other voices, the music from someone's phone, the ball games in the sand, the ice creams and little birds.

"You're going to get your shorts wet, Evelyn. You don't have your period, do you?"

But Evelyn has no time to be embarrassed or to listen because she's found what she's been looking for.

The only way to survive a whirlpool is to let yourself be dragged along by it. You can't try to stay afloat, or to swim or go back. You have to let it suck you up and sink you into its confusion, drag you along.

Evelyn moves deeper in until the water is up to her waist and her eyes are fixed on the little circle moving along, barely brushing the rope with the yellow buoys. The lifeguards use them to mark the limit beyond which the river starts to get dangerous. The sounds that reach her from the shore become part of a thick haze, but Evelyn can detect Marta's slightly alarmed voice asking her not to go out so far.

You have to hold air in your lungs so you can breathe. Because below the surface, there's another current that carries everything away to somewhere else. It's how you save yourself. Because that's what a whirlpool is: a force that devours you and spits you out when you least expect it. Evelyn, however, has been expecting it. She's almost reached it. Marta is on the shore and walks a little towards the water without taking her eyes off her daughter, who is now in up to her neck. Evelyn watches as the only part of the river that's moving around her approaches her. Then she inhales through her mouth until there's no more room in her lungs. She has to hurry up. She feels her mother's presence in the water. The time is now. Under the surface, she sinks her hand into the right pocket of her shorts and grabs Miss Laura's mobile. She tosses it into the centre of the whirlpool just in time and returns, running and pushing the water back with her hands. With all her strength.

ACKNOWLEDGEMENTS

My profound thanks to Gabriela Cabezón Cámara, my maestra, my friend. Without her, I'm not sure I'd be doing this sort of thing.

To the brilliant and generous women in her workshop with me: Belén López Peiró (for her urgent read the weekend before I turned the book in), Belén Longo, Carolina Cobelo, Charo Márquez, Constanza Viceconte, Celeste Contratti, Delfina Cabrera, Luciana Rabinovich, Mana Isla, Paula Amarilla, Paz Solís, Victoria Baigorri, Victoria García, Victoria Rodil.

To Ingrid Beck, my unconditional sister, the first reader of this story.

To Daniel Lagares, for the support, the love and the attentive reading that saved me from the kind of mistake one doesn't want to make.

To Liliana Escliar, who helped me with one eye that was clinical and the other loving.

To Alfredo Grieco y Bavio, for his impeccable and implacable reading.

To Gaby Esquivada, Gabriela Saidon, Hinde Pomeraniec, Laura Leibiker, Omara Alejandra Barra and Paula Pérez Alonso, because I'm not one for depriving myself of anything.

To Carolina Masariche, who lent me a hilarious slice of her life.

To Sergio Olguín, who doesn't know it, but who helped me out of a swamp when he recommended *Back to Blood*.

To the women at the Crespo Juniors cafeteria, who don't know it either, but whose laughter was a source of joy as I wrote.

To Glenda Vieytes, for her endless patience and generosity.

To Juan Pablo Bertazza, for his intelligent read and final edit.

To Julieta Obedman, who took a chance on my first novel in the middle of the crisis.

And to León, for his love.

AVAILABLE AND COMING SOON
FROM PUSHKIN VERTIGO